"Chhkk oot y-y guy," I whisper to Sofia through my teeth, shaking my hair back in his direction.

"Ooooooh. You want I should take the cupcakes and you go get his number?"

"No way!" I say. "You know my rule. No dating until the weddings are over."

"Jack!" Sofia protests.

"Not talking about it," I say firmly. "I'm telling you, there's a Wedding Curse, and I'm not losing any more guys to it. If I'm ever going to have a successful relationship, it's not going to be while this family is still in the throes of wedding madness."

TAMARA SUMMERS

Save the Date

HARPER TEEN

An Imprint of HarperCollinsPublishers

Library of Congress catalog card number:
2007930288
ISBN 978-0-06-136632-1

Typography by Sasha Illingworth
❖
First Edition

For all the brides I've ever known, none of whom were remotely as crazy as these. And for my own sister, the best bride ever.

—TTS

Prologue

I'm never having a wedding.

When I meet my dream boy—who will not be (a) boring, (b) obnoxiously fit, (c) an enormous role-playing dork, or (d) a Taiwanese model I barely know, like certain other people's husbands I could mention—my plan is to skip the whole inevitable wedding catastrophe. Instead we'll do it the old-fashioned way. I'll club him on the head, drag him off to Vegas, and marry him in a classy Elvis chapel, like our caveman ancestors would have wanted.

None of my five older sisters will have to be bridesmaids. In fact, they won't even have to come if they don't want to, except Sofia, who will be my maid of honor. And I won't force her to wear the most hideous dress I can find, because I, unlike most of my sisters, am a kind and thoughtful person with, I might add, a terrific sense of style.

Don't get me wrong; I love my sisters. I'm the baby of the family, so they've always taken care of me and treated me like their favorite toy when we were growing up. In fact, they were always super-nice to me, until they turned into brides. So despite the bridesmaid dresses they have forced me to wear and the weirdos they've married, I do love them.

It's just not safe to get married in this family, at least not if I, Jakarta Finnegan, bring a date to the wedding, which presumably I will to my own wedding. This is because the Finnegan family suffers from a terrible Wedding Curse, or at least I do. I don't know what we did to deserve it.

I didn't figure this out until after Wedding #2. I thought all the insanity at my oldest sister's wedding (#1) was normal behind-the-scenes craziness. When the best man got stuck in a snowstorm in Indiana—in JUNE—I was like, *Huh, weird,* and then when the organ player at the church came down with the mumps (in this century?), I thought it was strange, and sure, we were all a little freaked out by the flock of sea-gulls that crashed through the skylight in the reception hall during the cake cutting, but at no point did I think *Oops, my fault* or *Maybe I should uninvite Patrick to the wedding.* Afterwards, when this very first boyfriend I ever had broke up with me and fled in terror, it did cross my mind that maybe fourteen-year-old boys aren't cut out for nuptial ceremonies.

But it wasn't until the next wedding that alarm bells started to go off in my head. For instance, the day I asked my new boyfriend David to be my wedding date, the groom broke his wrist playing tennis and all three hundred invitations arrived back on our doorstep in a giant pile because they were missing two cents of postage. The day before the wedding, on the phone, was the first time I told David I loved him, and at that exact moment I got call waiting.

When I switched over, it was one of my uncles hysterically calling to tell us that the hotel where all the guests were supposed to stay had burned down. And *then*, on the way to the wedding, when I kissed David in the limousine, *lightning* struck the car in front of us, causing a massive six-car pile-up in which no one was hurt, but everyone involved in the ceremony was an hour late.

Lightning. Mumps. And *seagulls*. I'm telling you, I'm not crazy. This is a very real curse. And that's not even getting into the emotional wreckage afterwards with David, but I don't like to talk about that.

So you can see why I'm not crazy about the idea of having a wedding myself. Besides, all the good ideas have been taken. There's nothing else I could possibly do that hasn't been done before. That's what happens when you have five older sisters.

But I should start at the beginning—Victoria's bridal shower, where it all started to fall apart.

Or maybe I should go back to Sydney's and

Alexandria's weddings, so you get the big picture of what it's like to be a bridesmaid . . . over and over and over again.

Or maybe it goes back even farther than that, because to tell the truth, the trouble really started when my parents had Victoria and Paris only ten months apart.

Let's start with who I am (since I'm pretty sure that's not where anyone else would start). We'll get one thing out of the way right up front. My name is Jack. Under no circumstances will anyone call me Jakarta. It's not *my* fault that my parents are crazy and travel-obsessed, and none of us are going to encourage them by using my real name.

My parents are the Ken and Kathy of the Ken and Kathy's Travel Guide series. You must have seen the books—all about how to travel to fascinating places and have crazy adventures even with a pile of kids in tow. They travel all the time, always to exotic, fabulous, far-flung locales, and their house is full of wild foreign art and knickknacks. But it's one thing to hang an African mask on your wall or put down a

5

Peruvian llama rug. It's another thing altogether to name your children after the cities you've traveled to, don't you think?

Mine is by far the worst, of course. I mean, it figures; I'm the youngest, with five older sisters, so they had obviously run out of decent names for girls by the time I came along. I think they were hoping I'd finally be a boy so they could get the Santiago they always wanted.

My sisters don't have it so bad: Alexandria, Sydney, Victoria, Paris, and Sofia. Those could totally be normal-person names, couldn't they? Not like Jakarta. I mean, seriously.

I guess it could be worse. My name could be Tlaquepaque, or Irkutsk, or Pyongyang. Or, you know, Pittsburgh. Sometimes I flip through the atlas just to remind myself of all the names that would be worse than mine.

That's me. Looking on the bright side.

Alexandria, the oldest, is twenty-eight now. She's a lawyer, and she's tall and thin and blond and perfect-looking all the time. Sofia and I seriously can't believe we're related to her. She got married two years ago, to another lawyer, Harvey the Boringest Man on Earth. That was the wedding with the snowstorm and the mumps and the seagulls. The one where Patrick broke up with me.

Then there's Sydney, who's a year and a half younger. She's athletic and short and full of energy, and she's a pediatrician. She married her tennis instructor a year ago. When I say "obnoxiously fit"? You have no idea. Marco makes me tired just looking at him. Even when he's sitting at our kitchen table reading the newspaper, you can tell he's burning major calories. Their wedding was the one where the hotel burned down and lightning hit a car and David was a majorly enormous jerk.

After Sydney came Victoria and Paris, only ten months apart and about as different as two people can be. Victoria, our "romantic" sister, is willowy and pale, wears her hair long and flowing like a nymph in a Pre-Raphaelite painting, and is very sweet and quiet . . . or, at least she was until she became a bride-to-be. Paris, on the other hand, has bright red hair cropped close to her head, a nose ring, and a burning desire to be the world's most famous female glassblower. My mom says she's "an individual."

Paris was enough to keep my parents busy for four years. Personally, if I had a daughter like Paris, I wouldn't ever have sex again, just in case there was another one like her lurking in there. The world couldn't SURVIVE two Parises.

Luckily, what they got instead was Sofia, my twenty-year-old sister who is also my best friend and the biggest genius in the universe. She's graduating from college this year—she triple-majored and still finished in three years.

Then there's me. Recently turned seventeen. I have normal curly brown hair, shoulder-length, and normal gray eyes. I try not to make a fuss because I saw my parents endure Paris's wild teenage years and it didn't look like fun for any-one. By being a regular good kid, I get to do most-ly whatever I want, and there's a lot less shouting. Also, it's hard to stand out when I'm with my sisters. If I tried to be loud (or naughty), Paris would be louder (and much, much naughtier). If I tried to be sweet, Vicky would be sweeter. If I tried to be bossy, Alex . . . well, you get the idea. So I try to stay under the radar, and I try to be helpful, because once Mom told me: "Jakarta, honey, we love that you're such an easy child," and that's probably the only thing that she's never said about my sisters—even Sofia, who was too gifted to be easy. (And you know what's nice about being the easy child? I'm the one they still take on their travel excursions. Not making a fuss has gotten me to India and Egypt and Paraguay and Portugal, so even when Paris gets all the attention, I still think I'm winning.)

I'm not blond or super-fit or perfect. Not romantic, not "an individual," and definitely not a genius. So what am I? I'll tell you what: a bridesmaid.

It feels like I've been a bridesmaid for three years straight, and we're not even halfway through my sisters yet. Victoria's wedding is this summer and then Paris . . . well, we'll get to that in a minute.

Chapter One

It's a Saturday in early May, and Mom is organizing and hosting Victoria's bridal shower at this fancy tea room in town. It couldn't be more Victoria. All the chairs have big puffy flowered cushions on them and all the teacups come in different sizes with little matching plates—all covered in flowers, of course. When I walk in the front door, I nearly impale myself on a giant angel that takes up the entire foyer, its massive marble wings blocking the entrance to the tea room. It stares at me forbiddingly. Even the enthusiastic arrangements of fresh flowers piled on top of its head don't make it seem any friendlier.

"Can I help you?"

I jump and look around. As far as I can tell, I'm alone in this very pink room. I squint at the wallpaper, which looks like a rose garden went mad and tried to escape by climbing the walls. I kind of know how it feels.

"I said, can I *help* you?"

I turn slowly and look at the angel. It's definitely glaring at me. But it also definitely looks like it's made of marble. I glance around to make sure I'm alone and then lean toward it.

"Are you talking to me?" I whisper.

"*Ahem,*" says a sharp voice, and I suddenly realize it's coming from above the angel.

I look up. I stand on tiptoe. Impatiently, the person scoots some tall vases to the side so I can see her, and I realize that the angel is sort of a reception desk, with the welcome person standing on a step behind it and leaning over its head.

Although "welcoming" isn't exactly how she looks by this point.

"Um, hi," I say. "I'm here for the—um, the bridal shower."

"Which one?" Grandmother Grumpy snaps.

There's more than one? "Victoria Finnegan?" I say.

"Really?" says the old woman with, I think, unwarranted skepticism. It's true Victoria and I don't look much alike, and I also don't fit the spacey, hippie-skirt-wearing, Elvish-speaking mold of most of her friends. But hello, we *are* sisters, so yes, I do deserve to be here, Madame Grouchypants.

"My sister brought my mother over earlier," I say lamely, wondering if I should have come with Alex and Mom. I'd opted for the extra half hour of sleep instead, plus the bonus of getting to drive the car over by myself, which I can finally do now that I have my license instead of just a permit.

"Oh, there you are, Jakarta," my mother says, bustling into the lobby. I shoot the receptionist a fierce look to make sure she isn't laughing at my name. My mom and dad never remember to call me Jack, and I don't want to hurt their feelings by making a fuss about it. But they're the only ones who can get away with it.

"Did you bring the favors?" Mom asks, her voice already full of panic, even though I am clearly holding two giant shopping bags.

"Of course I did," I say. After spending the entire night wrapping translucent lace and lavender ribbons around lilac candles, I hardly think I'd then be dumb enough to leave them at home. Oh, and if you're curious about which of the other bridesmaids suffered through this along with me? None of them. Alex had too much work to do at the firm, Sydney was on call, Sofia was clever enough not to come home from college until this morning, and nobody's heard from Paris in about a week.

Don't worry, that's not unusual. She's a freewheeling crazy-artist type, after all, and she's actually sold a couple of big pieces so she can afford to do freewheeling crazy-artist-type things (especially since she still lives at home and doesn't pay rent, ahem). She usually leaves us notes like: "Absolutely MUST see Chihuly exhibit in Philadelphia. Be back Friday. Toodles!" or "Have fallen desperately in love

14

with baby panda. Off to re-create it as a vase. Call you from China!" The most recent one said cryptically: "Found something hotter than glass. Will share with you all next week. See you then!"

Mom takes the bags from me and sticks her nose in them, inspecting the candles to make sure I haven't crushed them on the way over.

"Where are your sisters?" she frets. "Paris and Sofia both promised they would be here before the shower started."

"There's still half an hour to go," I say. "Don't worry . . . Sofia will be here." That's about the best reassurance I can muster. Paris could easily be windsurfing in Australia for all we know. It would be fairly typical of her to forget Victoria's bridal shower. I've been getting this weird vibe that she's jealous of all the attention Vicky's getting, but Paris is too loud and flashy to let anyone know what she's really feeling. And seriously, has she met Vicky's fiancé? You'd have to be crazy to be jealous of Kevin. He is the world's weirdest guy.

"Alexandria is finishing the decorations, and Sydney is on her way with the cupcakes," Mom says anxiously. "I think. I hope she is—I didn't call to remind her—do you think she forgot?"

"You *did* call to remind her," I point out. "You called her this morning at seven o'clock, and you're lucky, because of all of us, I think Sydney's the only one who'd actually be up at that hour. Jogging or weight-lifting or throwing javelins or whatever."

"Yes, but then I meant to remind her again and I didn't. Maybe I should call her. She's supposed to bring the monogrammed lavender napkins, too . . . I'm sure she forgot those. Oh, I'd better call her."

This is why we hired a wedding planner for Victoria's wedding. Sydney tried to do her entire wedding herself, and it nearly made Mom's head pop off. For some reason navigating foreign countries doesn't faze her, but choosing between orchids and calla lilies sends her right out of her mind.

Speaking of our inexhaustible wedding planner, Carolina Trapelo, here she is now, appearing magically the way she always does when my mom's voice gets into that alarming upper register. Carolina's thick dark hair is piled on her head in a twist that looks both messy and elegant at the same time, and she is impeccably tailored, as always, in a suit that perfectly fits her sizable curves.

"Jack, *chiquita*, you look sooo beautiful today," she says, kissing both my cheeks. This is a blatant lie, as I am wearing a shapeless lemon yellow sundress—YELLOW—on my mother's strict instructions. It's one of Vicky's wedding colors, along with baby pink, baby blue, and lavender, any one of which would at least look better on me than yellow, but I learned way back during Alex's wedding that the path of least resistance is the one that gets me to the end of the reception with the least stress.

"And Kathy, darling, don't fret, I got the napkins and Sydney is right behind me with the cupcakes." She turns to wave out at the parking lot, and through the window I suddenly spot the most gorgeous guy I have ever seen.

He's leaning against a black hybrid car, wearing jeans, sunglasses, and a dark blue button-down shirt with the sleeves rolled up. His dark hair has just a hint of curl in it, and he's playing with a yo-yo. It's the first time I've ever seen someone make a yo-yo look sexy and mysterious.

As I'm watching him, Sydney's car pulls into the spot beside his. He glances up, but much to my approval, does not ogle my sister's toned biceps and evenly tanned legs. Instead he looks back down and spins the yo-yo around again.

I have to get out there. I have to get closer to the mystery dreamboat. True, I am not at peak hotness in this dress, but I'm not trying to get *his* attention. I just want to see if he really looks that much like a young Clive Owen from up close.

"I'll go help Sydney with the cupcakes," I say, dumping the bags of favors on the floor and zipping out the door before Mom can stop me.

I scoot up to Sydney as she is leaning into

her trunk, stacking three long flat boxes of cup-cakes on top of one another. Her dress is a little too vibrant to be "baby" pink, but I'd bet she doesn't own anything pastel, so it's close enough.

Sexy Yo-Yo Guy has really nice arms. Can you get really nice arms from lots of yo-yo-ing? He may or may not be looking at me through his sunglasses. And he does, in fact, look a bit like Clive Owen, without the five o'clock shadow and tired eyes. Not that I can see his eyes. It's just a guess.

"Oh, teriff," Sydney says, spotting me. "Hold out your arms." Sydney can be very brisk. I guess she's saving her energy for sports. I let her pile two boxes in my arms while I try to stare at Sexy Yo-Yo Guy without looking like I'm staring at him. The sunglasses are an unfair advantage, since I can't tell where he's looking.

"Careful, Jack," Sydney orders. "Keep them level so the frosting won't smush. Hey, look, it's Sofia."

I nearly fling the boxes into the air with

excitement, but I manage to restrain myself. Finally, the one sister I want to see is here—and just in time for me to share Sexy Yo-Yo Guy with her. Thank God she found an Ivy League college less than two hours away to go to, because I need at least a monthly dose of her sanity to handle living with Paris. I haven't seen her in three weeks because she's been working hard-core on her thesis. (Something involving physics and music. I know—*bwah?* Maybe I'll understand it once I get to college, which, thank God, is only a year away. I'm counting on college to be virtually wedding-free.)

"Jack!" Sofia cries happily as she bounds up to us, her dark curls bouncing. She's wearing lavender per Mom's instructions, and is carrying a silver gift bag. *Whoops.* How many of these stupid things do I have to go to before I remember to bring a present? Isn't staying up all night wrapping candles present enough? I ask you.

"I missed you!" Sofia says, giving me a half-hug around the boxes. "Hi, Sydney."

"Careful!" Sydney admonishes. "The cupcakes!" She leans back into the trunk to get the last box.

"Chhkk oot y-y gyy," I whisper to Sofia through my teeth, shaking my hair back casually in his direction.

Sofia, of course, understands what I'm saying right away. Her eyes flick over my shoulder and back so quickly there's no way he could have spotted it.

"Ooooooh," she murmurs. "You want I should take the cupcakes and you go get his number?"

"No way!" I say, blocking her move toward the boxes. "You know my rule. No dating until the weddings are over."

"Jack!" Sofia protests, but I'm already heading back to the tea room. She hurries to catch up with me. "Jack, you're being daft," she says. Sofia likes goofy words like "daft" and "impropriety" and "muddle." She continues, "What happened with Patrick at Alex's wedding was not the wedding's fault, it was Patrick's. Normal guys wouldn't be freaked out

21

by something like that."

"Oh, really?" I say. "Let's see. For starters, he had to see me in that horrendous red bridesmaid dress with the poofy hip and butt rosettes, which would never have happened if it hadn't been a WEDDING. Then he had to dance with me—terribly, I might add—in front of everyone because I was in the bridal party and Alex insisted—which, again, would never have happened if it hadn't been a WEDDING. Then the wedding singer made fun of him for wearing the same blue tuxedo as the waiters—also a uniquely WEDDING problem. And THEN Alex threw the stupid bouquet *right at me*—and I *caught* it! And of course Paris was immediately like, 'Ooooooh, Patrick, look out, I guess you guys are next, ooooh, I think you should get maaaaaaarried on the beach, that'd be romaaaaaaantic, oooooh.' To a fourteen-year-old guy! Of course he ran for the hills! And that's not even getting into the mumps and the seagulls."

Sofia rolls her eyes. "Yeah, because thinking that was your fault is totally crazy, Jack."

"Well, what about the guy you brought to Sydney's wedding? We haven't seen a trace of Ben since then, have we?"

"That was different." Sofia blushes. "He had to go back to Oxford."

"And then there's what happened with David at Sydney's wedding, which we are not talking about."

"But—"

"Not talking about it," I say firmly. "I'm telling you, Sofia, there's a Wedding Curse, and I'm not losing any more guys to it. Weddings scare boys, and that's all this family does nowadays. No." I shake my head. "If I'm ever going to have a successful relationship, it's not going to be while this family is still in the throes of wedding madness. And we're going to have a chaos-free wedding this time if I have to be celibate for the next three years."

"You're not going to wait all the way until *I* get married, are you?" Sofia asks in mock horror. "Because trust me, at the rate I'm going, you could be waiting a long time." Sofia hasn't dated

23

a lot of guys. Ben was the big Love of Her Life, according to her, and he was only in the country for six months. Mostly she spends a lot of time studying, which I find hard to understand. College guys are *muuuuuch* cuter than high school boys. Believe me, the selection at my high school makes it awfully easy to keep my not-dating resolution.

"We'll see," I say. "I was thinking maybe after Victoria's wedding I'd try again. I mean, I figure that should give me at least a couple of years before you and Paris turn into crazy brides—right?"

"Ooooh, yay!" Sofia says. "That means you'll be on the market again in about six weeks. Maybe we should tag and release Yo-Yo Guy so you can find him again when the wedding is over."

"That would be awesome," I say. "You keep a tracking device and a tranquilizer gun in your purse, don't you?"

"Or, you know," Sofia points out gently, "you could date a guy and *not* bring him to

Vicky's wedding." She holds the door open for me as I maneuver the cupcake boxes into the foyer. Grandmother Grumpy scowls at us over the angel and points down the hall to the left.

"Please," I say to Sofia. "You haven't seen the look in Vicky's eyes lately. If I so much as blink at someone, she asks if I want him to be my plus one. She nearly invited the guy from the coffee shop because I said he had a nice smile."

"Really?" Sofia says. "Is he cute?"

"He's like fifty years old!" I cry. "I meant that he reminds me of Grandpa! But she's got romance on the brain. Trust me, it'll be much safer for Yo-Yo Guy if I don't get him involved in all this."

Sofia giggles. We pass under a bower covered in fake roses and find ourselves in The Parlor That Strawberry Shortcake Threw Up. Just about everything is pink, or lacy, or pink *and* lacy. At the far end of the room, Carolina is helping Alex pin a pink CONGRATULATIONS, VICTORIA! banner to the swarming roses on the wallpaper.

"Well, maybe Yo-Yo Guy is more mature

than Patrick," Sofia says. "He's way hotter, for starters. Maybe he can handle Paris's sniping."

"Wait'll you see the bridesmaid dresses Vicky has picked out for us," I say. "You won't want to bring a plus one either. Hey, *are* you bringing someone?"

Sofia turns a really unusual shade of pink that I'm not sure I've ever seen on her before. "Maybe," she says. "Mom! Hi!"

"Thank goodness you're here," Mom says to her, taking the cupcake boxes from my arms. "I thought I'd have to run this whole thing by myself."

"Nice," I say. "Thanks, Mom."

"I mean all of you, thank goodness you're *all* here," she says lamely, but it's okay. Sofia's my favorite, too. I think she's everyone's favorite.

We follow Mom over to one of the tables, which appears to be covered in maybe five lace tablecloths, one on top of the other. The table next to it already has three presents on it—probably from Alex, Mom, and Carolina. Ms. Trapelo doesn't have to give Vicky a present, especially since she can't even stay for the shower (she has another wedding to run today), but she always treats her clients like they're family. While Mom starts arranging the cupcakes on a plate, chattering about the guest list, Sofia adds her gift bag to the pile, looks at the three presents, and then looks back at me.

I roll my eyes and knock myself on the head.

She taps her nose, pulls a pen out of her purse, and scribbles something on the card attached to the bag. I lean over and see that she's added AND JACK below WITH LOVE FROM SOFIA.

"Are you sure?" I mouth. Mom hasn't noticed any of this. She's still explaining to us which of Vicky's friends will be at the shower, as if we'll actually (a) remember and (b) want to talk to them.

"Of course," Sofia whispers. "No worries. Although if you'd like to chip in twenty bucks later, that'd be okay—starving college student and all." She smiles.

"You bet. Thanks, Sofia." Whew. I even have

27

twenty bucks, since I've been working two evenings a week all year at the ice cream parlor in town. You know what really helps a person fit into a bridesmaid dress? Not free ice cream, that's for sure. With Sofia off at college and my parents traveling half the time, it's a good way to keep busy and stay away from Paris, who has this strange notion that she's supposed to be "minding" me while Mom and Dad travel. At least until something more exciting comes up and she decides to disappear too, which happens pretty often. It's weird having the house to myself after years of it being full of sisters. I guess as much as I complain about it, I like having people around, and the ice cream parlor is always busy, even in the winter.

By two o'clock, there's still no sign of Paris. Sofia and I are not exactly shocked. But Victoria arrives right on schedule and does a pretty good job of pretending to be surprised. And there are plenty of Victoria-esque girls there: a few of the other teachers and a couple of parents from the elementary school where she teaches art, her team of role-playing friends, plus some long-haired leftover flower children that she befriended at a Renaissance festival. They all love the scones and the teacups and the cupcakes, and they demand long, detailed descriptions of her dress (I'll give you a hint: lace, lace, lace, and more lace).

We start with opening the presents, which takes FOREVER. It probably wouldn't be so bad except I can't have scones or tea while it's happening, because I'm supposed to be writing down everything Vicky is getting and who it's from. Alex is doing this, too, but she insists I do it as well so we can check each other's afterwards to ensure it's all correct. I think Alex sent a thank-you note for the wrong thing to someone at her bridal shower, which, by the way: Paris's fault, since this was her job then. Why anyone would put Paris in charge of anything is a mystery, but of course, that was our first wedding, and we've all learned a lot since then.

Okay, mainly we've learned not to ask Paris to do anything important. But seriously, it makes a big difference.

Sofia and Sydney, meanwhile, make a hat out of all the ribbons, which Vicky has to wear at the end. I make a mental note: Not only will I not be having a wedding, I will definitely not be having a bridal shower. Shapeless lemon yellow sundresses: fine. Big goofy ribbon hats: NO.

Most of the presents are lame flowery things from her registry or strange medieval-looking nightdresses. I'm pretty sure one of them involves chain mail, which almost makes me pity Kevin for a second. Sofia, of course, has picked out the perfect gift—it's a long white silk negligee, but with just enough lace and frills to match Vicky's taste while still being . . . you know, tasteful.

"OOOOOOOOOOH," Vicky gasps. "Thank you, Sofia! Thank you, Jack! It's beauuuuuutiful!"

Sofia winks at me. I'm pretty sure I owe her more than twenty bucks for saving my butt like that.

After all the presents are opened, I'm hoping

I can grab something to eat, but the scones are all gone, and we're not allowed to eat the cupcakes until we've played the party games that Alex has painstakingly organized. The first one involves a list of questions that Alex secretly e-mailed to Vicky's fiancé, Kevin.

Alex makes us all guess how many of the questions Vicky will answer the same way that Kevin did. I put "zero," because I'm unromantic like that, and also because I know that whoever "wins" gets a "prize" of a cake knife and big goofy plate with a cake painted on it. I ask you, what is a seventeen-year-old supposed to do with something like that? Take it to college with me? It'd just end up in Mom's pantry along with all the other dumb presents she refuses to throw away.

"All right," Alex begins, looking pleased with herself. Her chin-length blond hair is combed perfectly straight today, and she's wearing a baby blue pantsuit, which, despite matching Vicky's wedding colors, still looks very chic on her. She holds up the sheet of paper with the questions on it. "How many children are you and Kevin going to have?"

"Easy!" Vicky squeals. "Four!"

"That's what he said, too," Alex says with a hint of disapproval in her voice. She hides it well, but I spot the little shudder she gives. Alex is planning to postpone children until she's made partner in her firm, and even then she'll have one, which she'll hand over to a nanny and see only at holidays and graduations.

"And what," says Alex dramatically, probably imagining herself in a courtroom, "are you planning to call your children?"

"Ophelia, Drake, Desdemona, and Swann," Vicky says promptly. I nearly spray tea all over the pink upholstery of the couch. Sofia clutches my arm, pinching me hard to stop me from giggling.

"Close," Alex says. "All but one. Instead of Desdemona, he said Dragonella."

Oh my God. Sofia's shoulders start shaking, which doesn't help. If I crack up now, Vicky will probably kick me out of the wedding. Actually, that wouldn't be so bad; more likely she'll just make my bridesmaid dress worse, if that's possible. I close my eyes and try to keep a straight face by remembering the presidents in order.

"Dragonella!" Vicky hollers in a very unbride-like way. "That moron! He *knows* it's Desdemona but he always gets it wrong!"

"Not everyone loves Shakespeare as much as you, sweetheart," Mom says diplomatically.

"Well, he's getting better," Vicky says. "At least he's stopped saying Salmonella."

She says this without a trace of amusement. I literally have to grab the pillow next to me and stuff my face into it so I won't howl with laughter.

"Jakarta, are you all right?" Mom asks.

"Oh, yes, she's fine," Sofia says, patting my shoulder. "She's just overcome with emotion. Such a beautiful day. All so romantic. You know." There's a hysterical tremble in her voice so I know she's fighting back giggles too.

"That's so sweet!" Vicky says. "It *is* very romantic."

"Hmmm," says my mom, who knows me better than Vicky does.

"If you two were a famous couple from history or literature, who would you be?" Alex says.

"Oooooh," Vicky says thoughtfully. "Well, obviously it'd be from Shakespeare, so . . . Romeo and Juliet?"

"He said Aragorn and Arwen," Alex says with a puzzled expression. She also totally pronounces Aragorn wrong. "Did he make those up?"

"They're from *Lord of the Rings*!" Vicky squeals. "Oh my God, he's so right! That's *so* romantic!"

Sofia and I roll our eyes at each other (discreetly).

Alex keeps going through the questions, and I have to admit I'm pleased that Vicky doesn't get them all right. Too much thinking alike makes a couple really weird, in my opinion. Alexandria and Harvey, for instance, are really into politics and law and talking about current events, but they have exactly the same opinion on everything, so their conversations end up being EVEN MORE BORING than you'd think they could possibly be—not that I ever have high hopes for conversations about politics and law and current events.

Vicky and Kevin seem like they have that one-brain syndrome sometimes, too, but I think she's a lot smarter than he is (I mean, Salmonella?). And at least they have some different interests—she's in a book club and takes jewelry-making classes, while he's on a fencing team (seriously) and claims to be designing the world's most complicated board game with his best man. Something about dragons and wizards, I'm sure you'll be shocked to hear.

Sydney and Marco, on the other hand, argue constantly, but at least they're fun to listen to.

After the questionnaire game—which, by the way, Sydney wins, so have fun with that cake plate, sis—we are *still* not allowed to eat cupcakes, because first we have to divide up into teams, pick someone to be our model, and make wedding dresses out of toilet paper and safety pins.

The good news: Sofia is on my team.

The bad news: So is Vicky's maid of honor, Lucille. Who seriously thinks I'm, like, nine years old, or something.

"Ooooh, let's have Jackie be our model!" she chirps. "Won't that be fun for you, sweetie?"

"Oh, no, that's okay," I try to demur. "I think you'd be a much better model."

"Puh-*lease*!" she exclaims. "*I* am like a fashion *mogul* over here. I could so *totally* be on *Project Runway*. We definitely need my skills on the *design* side." This woman, by the way, is wearing bright purple leggings under a long flowery dress with a Peter Pan collar. Enough said.

"Besides," one of the others points out, "you're the smallest. The toilet paper will go further that way." She's wearing a tag that says: "Hi! I'm <u>Mindy</u>! I know Vicky from <u>my son is in her art class</u>!"

This is why I am wrapped in yards and yards

of toilet paper, completely trapped, when Paris sweeps in to make her grand announcement.

It happens just after Mom bustles over to us, blinking nervously. "I *wish* I knew where your sister was," she says. "If she were here, we'd have even teams. This is *so* like Paris."

"Did somebody say my name?" a voice hollers from the doorway right behind us. Paris is standing there with her arms up in a "Ta da!" pose, her bright red hair clashing furiously with the pink wallpaper, her nose ring glittering in the lamplight. It's a little suspicious. If it wouldn't be too unsisterly of me, I'd suspect she'd been standing outside the doorway this whole time, waiting for someone to say her name so she could make a truly dramatic entrance.

"I'm heeeeeeeeeeeeee-re!" Paris singsongs. "The party may now begin!"

Vicky is turning pink. If she weren't also swathed in long strands of toilet paper, I think she might have stormed over and shoved Paris back out the door.

"My party began *two hours* ago," she says

icily. I can't exactly blame her. Paris has a way of sucking all the limelight in the room over to her corner. You'd think Vicky's bridal shower would be the one occasion where Vicky could be center stage instead, but I'm afraid that's not to be.

"I'm sorry, Vicky dear," Paris trills. "But I have *such* exciting news, I just couldn't *wait* to share it with everyone."

Uh-oh. "This bodes ill," Sofia whispers to me.

"Paris, couldn't you save your news until after Vicky's shower?" Mom tries, but Paris steamrolls right over her the way she always does.

"I want you all to meet . . . Jiro!" she says, and stands back with a flourish.

"EEEEEEEEEEEE!" Lucille shrieks. "There's a BOY! A BOY at the bridal shower! That's not allowed! Get him out, get him out!"

For once, I find myself agreeing with Lucille. I mean, I am still wrapped in toilet paper. And there aren't enough cupcakes for an extra guest. Oh, and? The guy standing sheepishly behind Paris, bowing and nodding, is, like, *smolderingly* good-looking. I am not kidding. He's like that guy Jin on *Lost* to the power of a hundred. I'm a little bit shocked that this guy and Sexy Yo-Yo Guy can be within twenty miles of each other without setting the world on fire.

"Paris . . ." Mom says weakly.

Jiro smiles a million-watt smile, bows again, and says something in Chinese. (Or maybe Taiwanese? Japanese? How would I know?)

"Jiro is from Taiwan. He's a model," Paris announces proudly. "And we . . . are getting married!"

Chapter Two

Mom actually faints. One moment she is gaping at Paris, and the next she is lying on the floor moaning softly.

"Mom!" we all cry. Sofia gets to her first, of course. I am in the midst of a moral quandary: leap to Mom's aid, or preserve the integrity of the toilet-paper dress? I mean, is the bridal shower going to continue? Are we still going to finish the game? Is Lucille going to stab me with a safety pin if I jump off my stepstool pedestal and tear my dress?

By the time these thoughts have floundered through my head, Mom is surrounded by Sofia, Alex, Sydney, Paris, and Vicky anyway. As usual, there is no need for me, so I stay perched right where I am, trying to look inconspicuous.

"Look what you did!" Vicky yells at Paris.

"I didn't do anything!" Paris yells back.

"You ruined everything! You deliberately ruined my shower! You . . . you selfish wench!" (Victoria is, um, not so much with the swearing.)

"*Me*, selfish?" Paris shouts. "I'm in *love*! Why can't you be happy for me, huh? Haven't I been supportive of *your* stupid wedding?"

"I knew it!" Vicky screams back. "I knew you were jealous of me! Well, this is priceless, Paris. I should have known you'd pull a stunt like this!"

"A stunt like what?" Paris is really having fun now. She would be the perfect candidate for one of those yelling-yelling-drama-drama reality shows. She did try out for *The Real World* once, but I think she scared the producers too much for them to cast her. THAT should tell you something.

"Forcing some random guy to marry you just so you can steal my thunder! Does he even speak *English*, Paris?"

From the fixed smile on poor Jiro's face, I'm guessing the answer to that question might be no.

"We don't have to speak the same language to know we're in love!" Paris hollers.

"Would you both shut up?" Alex snaps. "Mom, are you okay?"

"We need a wet washcloth," Sydney says briskly. "And we should keep her head elevated." Sofia jumps up and runs off to the bathroom.

"Smelling salts!" Vicky suggests frantically, drawing on the vast medical expertise she's picked up from reading too much Charles Dickens. She'll probably recommend leeches next.

"Or a cupcake," I offer. "I bet a cupcake would help." Nobody hears me.

Sofia runs back in with wet paper towels, which Sydney uses to dab Mom's forehead and temples.

"I'm all right," Mom says, blinking and sitting up. "It's okay, I'm fine."

"Jeez, Mom," Paris says. "I know he's hot, but even I didn't faint the first time I saw him."

She grins in what she thinks is a charming way.

"Get out," Victoria snarls at Paris. "I want you *out* of my bridal shower."

"You can't throw me out!" Paris cries. "I'm one of your bridesmaids!"

Vicky stands up with an expression that for some reason makes me think of Voldemort in those Harry Potter movies. "Not anymore, you're not," she says coldly.

All of her friends gasp in horror. Throwing a bridesmaid out of the wedding party! How scandalous!

"But Vicky," Lucille whispers, "don't you have six groomsmen? Won't that make the numbers uneven? Think of the asymmetrical photographs!"

"I don't care," Vicky says, and everyone gasps again.

"Victoria, sweetheart, let's think about this," Mom says, trying to pull her down on one of the couches. Vicky tugs her hand free.

"No!" she snaps. "Paris is always spoiling everything! I won't let her ruin my wedding,

43

too. Come on, Lucille."

Vicky tosses her hair back and storms out the front door, right past Jiro without even glancing at him, and that takes fortitude, because did I mention he's hot? It's a very dramatic moment, only slightly marred by the long ribbons of toilet paper that are still wrapped around her arms and torso. Lucille squeaks with excitement and scuttles after her, and most of Vicky's friends file out after them, chattering loudly.

"Wait!" I cry. "Don't forget your favors! Take candles, take candles!" A few of them actually hear me and snatch candles from the table by the door, but I can see we're going to have a giant stack of them left that Mom will have to store somewhere in our house for, probably, ever. Hurrah.

"FINE!" Paris yells after Vicky. "I didn't want to be in your STUPID WEDDING ANYWAY! And you DEFINITELY WON'T GET TO BE IN MINE! WHICH WILL BE WAY BETTER THAN YOURS! SO THERE!"

Alex and Sydney are on either side of Mom

on the couch, fanning her with gift cards. Sofia is practically wringing her hands; she can't stand it when people fight, which makes you wonder how she survived living with Paris for so long. Paris stomps over to Jiro, grabs his face, and kisses him hard. He blinks a few times in astonishment, then has the grace to look embarrassed.

"I don't care what anyone thinks," Paris announces. "I love Jiro, and I'm going to marry him. In three months. On the beach. And it's going to be the best wedding *ever*."

"Oh, shut up, Paris," Alex snaps. "Don't you ever think of anyone but yourself?"

"Girls," Mom says weakly.

"Seriously!" Sydney chimes in. "Do you know how much work we all put into this? God, Paris!" As far as I know, the "work" Sydney put in was picking up the cupcakes, which if you ask me, doesn't compare to wrapping stupid candles for no reason all night long, or addressing and stuffing shower invitations, or helping Mom buy tablecloths and flower arrangements. Honestly, it's a miracle I'm not flunking my junior year, considering how much time I spend on my sisters' weddings instead of on homework.

Not that I'm complaining, of course. Yaaaaaay weddings. Go true love, woo.

"Oh, where is Carolina when you need her?" Mom says helplessly. Which isn't really fair, because usually Carolina is right here when we need her, but she does have other weddings to run now and then.

"Carolina!" Paris says. "I love her! She can plan my wedding, too. I'm sure she'll find it way more fun than planning Vicky's boring extravaganza."

"We should check on Victoria," Mom says, trying to stand up.

"I'll go," Sydney says, pushing Mom firmly back down. "She's probably gone back to her apartment. I'll make sure she's all right."

"Thank you, Sydney," Mom says.

"Make sure *Vicky's* all right!" Paris shrills loudly as Sydney trots out of the room and down the hall. "Doesn't anyone care about *me*? Doesn't anyone want to *congratulate* me on my *fantastic* news? Doesn't anyone even want to say hi to Jiro, who's going to be a *member* of this *family* soon?"

Jiro hears his name and smiles again. I do feel sorry for him, so I wave, and he waves back.

"I think you care about yourself enough for everyone," Alex snaps. "Come on, Mom, I'm taking you home."

"But—" Mom protests. "The presents . . . the favors . . . the mess . . ." It is a giant mess in here. There's wrapping paper everywhere, piles of boxes, plates with half-eaten scones, and teacups scattered on all the tables. Not to mention discarded mountains of toilet paper all over the place.

"It's okay," Alex says soothingly to Mom. "Jack will take care of it." She shoots me a look full of daggers before I can object.

"I *would* like to lie down," Mom says. "Are you sure you don't mind, Jakarta?"

They all look at me, standing up on the stepstool with toilet paper wrapped tightly around my legs and hips and draped across my

47

shoulders. I think Lucille was going for some kind of mermaid look.

I force a smile. "No, that's totally fine. Go ahead, Mom, I'll be right behind you."

"I'll stay and help," Sofia says loyally. Have I mentioned that I love her?

Alex supports Mom to her feet. At the door, Mom pauses and holds her hand out to Jiro. "It's—it's very nice to meet you," she says kindly. No matter how flustered she gets, her maternal instincts always win.

He says something in Taiwanese with a little bow, pressing her hand in his. She smiles and answers in his language, which makes him smile broadly.

"What did you say?" Paris asks.

"He said we have a charming family," Mom says. (Alex snorts.) "And I wished him luck. He's going to need it."

"What does *that* mean?" Paris snaps.

"We'll talk about this at home," Mom says sternly. "Without subjecting this poor boy to any more squabbles. I'll see you there in half an hour." She points at Paris, and then lets Alex escort her out the door.

Now it's only me, Sofia, Paris, and poor Jiro left amidst the wreckage of the shower.

"Sofia?" I say. "A little help?" She comes over and starts unpinning me.

"WELL," Paris says dramatically. "I NEVER." She flounces over to the cupcake table, seizes an enormous cupcake covered in pink icing, and flops down on the couch. "Come here, Jiro," she says, patting the couch beside her. He obediently follows her over and sits down, then holds her cupcake wrapper while she stuffs the whole thing in her mouth.

"So, Paris," Sofia says, "um . . . where did you guys meet?"

"New York," Paris says around a mouthful of crumbs. "Remember that modeling shoot I went to? With Marc, who paid me to take some of the photographs and help with the costuming? Ha—when I saw Jiro, I was like, I know *exactly* what he should wear . . . nothing! Right? Am I right?" She pats Jiro's shoulder proudly, like he's one of

49

her brassy metal sculptures. Boy, I'm glad he has no idea what she's saying.

"New York?" I say. "Wasn't that only, like, two months ago?"

"Yup." Paris throws her arms around him. "It was love at first sight. We've been in Miami for the last week—he had a shoot down there—and one night I guess he realized how much he loves me and he just . . . proposed!"

"How do you know?" I asked.

"How do I know what?"

"How do you know he proposed?" Sofia takes out the last safety pin and I jump off the stepstool in a cloud of toilet paper, shaking myself free. Sofia digs a trash bag out from under one of the tables and starts to fill it, but I head for the cupcake table first. No way am I doing this without a cupcake, especially since I haven't eaten anything at all yet today. At least there is one (and only one) upside to Paris crashing the shower like this: Now there are a ton of leftover cupcakes.

"Whatever," Paris says. "I could tell. Trust

me, Jack, if you ever fall in love, you'll see what it's like. We don't need words to understand each other."

I perch on the table, peel the wrapper off a chocolate cupcake, and study Jiro. I wonder if he has any idea what's going on, or if he's going to wake up one morning in August, get stuffed into a tuxedo, and find himself on a beach reciting vows in a foreign language. I wonder if Paris's wedding day will turn into a wacky chase scene. That would be sort of fitting.

"Is this a green card thing?" Sofia asks. "I mean, do you have to get married so quickly because he needs to stay in the country?"

"No," Paris says, looking offended. "We're getting married 'so quickly' because we *love* each other! Not that I expect you guys to understand that. But no, there's no green card thing. Jiro was born in the States, so he's a citizen, even though he grew up in Taiwan. Right, Jiro? American citizen?" she says loudly and slowly.

"Ah, yes," he says, nodding agreeably. "American." Man, his teeth are ridiculously straight.

51

I finish my cupcake and help Sofia clean up. Paris, of course, stays right where she is. She lies down in Jiro's lap, and he starts running his fingers through her short hair.

"So, three months from now?" I say. "That's your plan?"

"Yup," Paris says. "In August, on the beach. And you two are going to be my only bridesmaids, so there."

"What?" I say, horrified. "Why? I mean . . . yay?"

"Because you two are the only ones who've supported me in this," Paris says. I give Sofia a look that says, *We have? How were we stupid enough to do that?* "Obviously Vicky and Alex and Sydney are too selfish to be happy for me, but here you guys are, being nice, like always. We don't need anyone else, right, girls? It'll be awesome, just the three of us. Screw the older sisters. Hags."

Well, that's awesome. Thanks a lot, toilet paper game. If I hadn't been stuck here, maybe I could have stormed out with the others, and then I wouldn't have to be one of Paris's bridesmaids.

Paris grabs another cupcake and murmurs sweet nothings at Jiro while she feeds it to him. I follow Sofia to the far corner of the room, where we start taking down the banner.

"Wow, we're so *lucky*," Sofia whispers sarcastically.

"Remind me to be more negative in the future," I mutter to Sofia.

"Oh, no," Sofia says, catching my arm. "This doesn't mean—you're not still going to stick to your vow, are you?"

"Um, I totally am," I say. "Please, are you kidding me? Paris's wedding is going to be the most insane of all of them. No *way* am I going to date in the middle of all that! I can wait until August."

"But what about faboo dreamy Yo-Yo Guy?" Sofia says. "What if he can't wait until August?"

"*C'est la vie*," I say. "Anyway, it doesn't matter. It's not like I'm ever going to see him again."

But I was wrong. I did see him again, much sooner than I thought . . . and in the most unexpected place.

Chapter Three

We have cupcakes for dinner that night, because Mom is too upset to cook. We also have cupcakes for breakfast the next morning, because Mom and Dad are too busy fighting with Paris to stop us.

"This is a great idea," I say, selecting my fourth cupcake from the box—this one vanilla with lavender icing.

"I agree," Sofia says, although she's only on her second. We are still in our pajamas; hers are cute and matching, blue with little suns all over them, while mine are a pair of flannel pants and a tank top. My bare feet swing against the bars of the tall stools around the kitchen island, where we are hiding from the hollering in the living room.

"WHAT ARE YOU THINKING?" my dad shouts in the background. "YOU DON'T EVEN KNOW THIS GUY!"

"I know I *love* him!" Paris screams back.

"Well, I hope you're not expecting us to pay for this baloney!" Dad yells.

"I'm not ASKING YOU TO!" Paris hollers. "We don't need MONEY because we have LOVE!"

"Does it have to be this summer?" Mom pleads. "You know your father and I have been planning a research trip to Costa Rica in July."

"WHAT'S MORE IMPORTANT?" Paris bellows. "YOUR DAUGHTER'S HAPPINESS OR STUPID, STUPID COSTA RICA?"

"At least stupid, stupid Costa Rica keeps food on the table!" my dad bellows back.

This is pretty much the same argument they've been having since we got home yesterday.

"You know what's so great about this idea?"

I say, waving my cupcake at Sofia. "The fact that we're getting fitted for our bridesmaid dresses this afternoon. I can't think of anything that could prepare us better for that ordeal than eating eight cupcakes in a row."

"Eight?" Sofia says admiringly. "I'd like to see you try."

"Is that a dare?" I ask. "What'll you give me if I do it?"

Sofia taps her chin thoughtfully. "Hmm, let's see . . . okay, if you really eat eight cupcakes right now, I'll take charge of planning Paris's bachelorette party."

"Seriously? But what if Mom and Dad win and Paris doesn't get married?"

My sister laughs. "Jack, when do Mom and Dad ever win a fight with Paris?"

Good point. And the last thing I want to do is plan Paris's bachelorette party. Shudder. I stuff the rest of the cupcake in my mouth and grab four more.

Half an hour later, Mom wants to know why I don't want pizza for lunch. Also, why

I'm lying on the floor of the den clutching my stomach.

"I think she's full," Sofia says innocently from the couch. "We had a big breakfast."

"Well, I hope so," Mom says. "Don't forget we have the dress fittings today. I hope you're not starving yourself for that, because that would be very unhealthy, and I don't want you complaining that you're hungry in the middle of the appointment."

"Don't worry. I won't," I mumble into the carpet. Our Irish setter, Dublin, trots over and starts trying to lick off my face, but I don't have the strength to push him away. I feel like I've eaten lead weights instead of cupcakes.

"Girls?" Mom calls from the kitchen. "What happened to all the cupcakes? Wasn't there another box of them?"

Sofia and I dissolve into giggles. Paris flounces into the room and throws herself down on the couch beside Sofia.

"What's so funny?" she demands.

"Nothing," Sofia says.

I roll over and smile sweetly up at Paris. "Sofia has volunteered to plan your bachelorette party," I say. "She's SO excited about it."

"Oh my gosh!" Paris shrieks at top volume. "That's awesome! Sofia, you're the best!" She throws her arms around Sofia, who gives me a death glare over Paris's shoulder. "This is going to be the best bachelorette party ever! I'm so glad you guys are supporting me—I'm glad SOMEBODY is," Paris announces loudly. "Maybe later I can tell you some of my ideas for the party, Sofia. There's only, like, ten people I want to invite, but they're all REALLY important so we just have to work out our schedules so that EVERY SINGLE ONE of them can be there. Okay? Awesome! I can't wait!"

She leaps up again and bounds out of the room. Sofia raises an eyebrow at me.

I pat my stomach contentedly. "Tooooootally worth it."

Esme, the woman at the bridal shop who is adjusting all our bridesmaid dresses, is Not

Pleased to hear that one of the bridesmaids has been replaced. Yes, that's right—Vicky went home and immediately picked another one of her friends to replace Paris. Kelly is pale and quiet, and I have a feeling Vicky chose her only because she's the same size as Paris, so the dress wouldn't need much adjusting. Still, Esme is Not Pleased.

"And you," she says, poking my stomach, "what you been eating?"

"Cupcakes," I say with a straight face. "Lots and lots of cupcakes."

"This is not joke," she says, wagging her finger in my face. "No more eating until wedding." Sofia gives me a scandalized look. Esme is lucky my mom is in the other back room with Vicky and Lucille, or she'd be getting the patented Kathy Finnegan eating-disorder talk. Trust me, none of the girls in my family will ever have a problem with eating, if only because none of us wants to hear that lecture ever again.

"I start with you," Esme says to Sydney. "Dress should fit you perfect. I hope you all bring shoes!" She sweeps my second-oldest sister behind a curtain to strip and measure her.

Alex sighs and snaps open her briefcase, pulling out some files. Sofia retrieves *Pride and Prejudice* from her purse, which she is reading for about the tenth time. I know I should be studying *Catcher in the Rye* for the final in two weeks, but instead I let my gaze wander around the dress store. There are two other brides out in the front room, on the other side of the half-drawn curtain from us, each with a cluster of people around them giving opinions. One of them, with frizzy red hair, is trying on a perfectly hideous ballgown style that makes her look like a marshmallow on steroids. Carolina Trapelo sweeps in the front door.

"Hello, darling Finnegans," she says to all of us, dropping air kisses over our heads and patting me on the cheek. "Is the beautiful bride here?"

"Vicky's in the back with Mom," Sofia says, pointing. "They're trying to pick out a veil."

"A veil, tsh!" Carolina says. "It's perfectly

clear that for Victoria, a flower headdress is the only way to go. Jack, dear, would you please pick out the most flowery tiaras you can find from the front display and bring them back to us? I'll see how your mother's doing."

She sweeps away, and I obediently get up to go pick out tiaras. I like Carolina, and she has yet to give me anything really annoying to do.

And then, as I step toward the tiara display, all of a sudden . . . I see him.

Yes, *him*.

He has no yo-yo today. He's sitting on a bench in the corner, right beside the tiara display, reading something. As I get closer I can see that it's a graphic novel, and my heart goes pitter-pat. Not that I'd be turned off if he was reading *Ulysses* or whatever, but I love comic books. Not in a collect-'em-all, buy-the-figurines, original-packaging-don't-touch kind of way. I just like reading them.

He's also not wearing his sunglasses, so I can see that his eyes are green and even nicer than Clive Owen's.

See, now I don't have a choice. I *have* to go over there. I *have* to stand about four feet away from him. It's my duty as a bridesmaid. And I am a *very* dutiful bridesmaid.

The tiaras are arranged on long shelves against the wall. I put on a studious expression, but I'm not really looking at them. I'm trying to figure out if he's looking at me, and I have a weird feeling that he is.

Suddenly a horrible thought hits me. What is he doing in a bridal store? What would any guy be doing in a bridal store? Does he have a weird wedding-dress fetish or something? Or . . . surely he's not getting married. I sneak a peek at him. He looks no older than eighteen, but looks can be deceiving. *Oh, God, I hope he's not marrying marshmallow girl,* I think despairingly. Maybe he's just her brother or something. Most brides wouldn't drag their grooms along to look for dresses, right? This girl might, though. She looks pretty crazy.

"Hey."

When he speaks, I'm so startled, I actually

turn around to see if it's someone behind me before I realize it's him talking. He has a very cute smile.

"Hey," I say back. He just keeps smiling at me. "Um," I add, "come here often?"

"You'd be surprised," he says. Hmm. That's worrying. Maybe my fetish theory is right. "How about you?" he asks.

"Unfortunately, yeah, pretty often," I say.

"Ah," he says knowingly. "So how many times have you been married?"

"Ha ha," I say. "Only twice, sheesh."

That throws him for a second. He tilts his head at me. "Seriously?"

"Yeah, really rich old guys, but they both died," I say, widening my eyes, "under mysterious circumstances. Weird, huh?"

He grins again. "You almost had me for a minute."

I wish I had you! This guy might even be worth breaking my vow for. Maybe I can do it if I keep him far, far away from all the wedding craziness. "Man, how old do you think I am?" I ask.

"Not that old," he says. "Like, definitely no older than thirty."

I put my hands on my hips. "You know, most guys at least tell me their names before insulting me."

"Leo," he says, holding out his hand. *Oh my God, I'm going to touch his hand!* I shake it, trying to stop myself from smiling so much. *Oh my God, I'M TOUCHING HIS HAND!*

"I'm Jack," I say. "My sister's getting married." I gesture to the back, hoping that he'll be like, "Oh, yeah, mine too."

Instead he says, "Are you one of her bridesmaids?"

"Oh, yeah," I say. "This is time number three."

"For your sister?"

"For me," I say, laughing. "I mean, third sister to get married, third wedding I have to be a bridesmaid in."

"Have to be?" he echoes. "Don't you like it?"

"Sure," I say. "Especially the fantastic dresses. Or wait, maybe it's running crazy errands for

64

my sisters for months, like 'Trim these calla lily stems to exactly nine inches long—EXACTLY,' or 'Go buy me a new inkjet printer cartridge and five yards of burgundy ribbon right this instant.' Or having them freak out at me on the big day— that's fun, too."

"Wow," he says. "That's specific. I guess you've been doing this awhile."

"And then there's number four, our most crazy sister, at the end of the summer. We're really looking forward to that."

"Ohhh," he says. "You must be one of the Finnegans."

I stare at him. How on earth has the Hottest Guy in the Universe heard of my ridiculous family? Even if he reads travel books for fun or something, that doesn't seem to be what tipped him off.

"Jack, darling," Carolina trills, bustling up. "Did you find any flower tiaras? Oh, I see you've met my son Leo."

Leo winks at me, and my heart sinks. He's the wedding planner's son?

Then there's no way I can keep him away from my family's wedding insanity. Which means, no way I can date him. If I try, the Wedding Curse will strike, something terrible will happen, and he'll get scared off anyway.

"Leo's helping me this summer, which is going to be a busy one for your family." Carolina wags her finger at me. "Paris called me last night, and luckily I'm available for the weekend she wants. She has a lot of ideas, that one!"

"Somehow that doesn't surprise me," I say wryly.

"But right now the focus is Victoria," Carolina says, clapping her hands. I like that she says that. Victoria's not my favorite sister these days, either, but I still think she deserves to be the star of her own wedding. "Which tiara do you think, Jack? I'm trying to stop her from choosing the most hideous veil."

"Oh—I don't know," I say, looking at the shelf again. Just then we all hear Lucille screeching from behind one of the curtains.

Something about looking like a whale in her dress.

"I'll help Jack, Mom," Leo says, standing up. "Sounds like you've got a situation."

"Dear dear dear," Carolina says, bustling away again.

"Whew," I say. "I don't envy your mom. I'd hate to be a wedding planner."

"I think it's kind of fun," Leo says. "But she's paying me for this. I'd probably find it less fun if I had to do it for free."

"Shyeah," I say. I'm feeling a bit less witty now that he's standing literally inches away from me. His arm is practically brushing mine. He's looking at the shelves of tiaras with intense interest, but I wonder if he's noticed how close we're standing.

"So tell me about Victoria," Leo says. "What kind of wedding is she having?"

"The key word is flowers," I say. "And the other key word is Renaissance festival."

"Yeeee, really?" Leo says. "I mean, ahem, sorry, professional face: That sounds SO lovely.

I'm sure it's going to be the most BEAUTIFUL day."

I giggle. "Think lace and pastel colors and Celtic harps, and you'll be on the right track."

"All right," he says. "Maybe . . . this one?" He pulls out a tiara that's got silver daisies woven along it. It's totally perfect.

"Wow—yeah, that's really Vicky," I say admiringly.

"Try these two as well," he says, taking down two more that have flower motifs. "But she might want to skip the veil/tiara thing altogether and just wear flowers in her hair. I've seen a couple of brides do that, and it sounds like it would match her wedding."

Aha, I think regretfully. *He's gay.* Well, that was a short-lived fantasy.

"My mom's been doing this a long time," he explains, a little sheepishly.

"Okay," I say, taking the three tiaras. Our hands brush as he passes them over, and I feel a weird tingle of excitement shiver across my skin. "Thanks." I smile at him, then turn to carry them back to Victoria.

"So," he says quickly, "um . . . how's your bridesmaid dress? Do you hate it?"

"Oh, totally," I say. "It's horrendous."

"Can I see it?" he says charmingly. "I might be able to help."

"Definitely not," I say, grinning at him. "You *definitely* can not see me in this dress."

He grins back, and I have to scamper behind the curtains before he sees how much I'm blushing.

"OMG," I whisper to Sofia. "Sexy Yo-Yo Guy is here."

"He is?" she says, bolting up out of her seat. "Where?" I seize her before she can poke her head out of the curtain.

"Don't look," I hiss. "But guess what—he's Carolina's son."

"WHAT?"

"Shhhhhhhhhhhh!"

"You most certainly do *not* look like a whale, Lucille," Carolina's voice says patiently from the back room.

"I doooooooo!" Lucille howls. "My belly fat is sticking out all over the place!"

"Did you talk to him?" Sofia whispers excitedly. I see Alex giving us a suspicious glance.

"Yes—tell you later," I whisper back. "I have to take these to Vicky."

"Good luck with that," Sofia jokes. "She's in a bit of a snit about Lucille's tantrum."

Uh-oh. I sidle into the back room where Vicky is slouching in an armchair, fully outfitted in her bridal regalia, with her arms crossed and a scowl on her face. Lucille is standing on the pedestal in front of the mirror, with my mom and Carolina flitting anxiously around her.

"I think you look fine," Vicky snaps.

"But looooooooook," Lucille whines, poking her stomach.

All right. It's probably time for me to describe Victoria's choice of bridesmaid dress. But first let me start by giving you some context—that is, by describing the last two bridesmaid dresses that I had to wear. That way you can appreciate the true horror of the relentless fashion crimes being perpetrated on me.

Alex's wedding was a really traditional, classic affair, in a church, with pretty much everything you'd expect from the world's two most boring people. Except for her bridesmaid dresses, which I don't think any other bride has ever inflicted on her friends. She made us wear these strapless A-line red satin dresses—sounds okay so far, right? But for *no apparent reason*, these dresses came with giant poofy rosettes sewn on them—one on the left boob, one on the right hip, a whole row around the hem at the bottom, and three across the butt. We looked like extras from *Attack of the Killer Tomatoes*, if the tomatoes had invaded a wedding and exploded all over the bridesmaids.

Alex was like, "Ooh, Jack, it's so pretty on you! Wow! You can totally wear it to your prom!"

Yeeeeah. Apart from the fact that I was fourteen at the time of the wedding, so my prom was still three years away, there was pretty much no way I was ever going to wear that dress again.

For Sydney's wedding, she tried to be really different from Alex. It was in a museum, she wore a light pink sheath, and everything was sleek and modern . . . except the bridesmaid dresses. Something happens to brides, I'm telling you. She picked this god-awful two-piece vibrant pink ensemble with dark burgundy horizontal stripes, ruffles, pleats, AND . . . shoulder pads. I mean, REALLY.

Guess what she said about it? "Ooh, Jack, it's sooo cute! You can totally wear it to your prom!"

I'm really glad they'll both be long out of the house by the time my prom finally rolls around next year.

And now there's Victoria's wedding. Esme hustles into the room holding my dress. For starters, it is long—Vicky wants them to drape on the floor as we walk, even if that means they get caught on our high heels. She's been fighting with Esme about this for weeks. Vicky wants us to look like "woodland nymphs." Esme thinks we're going to have a six-bridesmaid pileup on the garden stairs, and that it goes against every rule of dressmaking not to hem the dresses above our feet.

As you can imagine, I side with Esme on this one, despite her unfortunate stance on eating.

In addition, the dresses are a pale grassy green with a pattern of eNORmous pink and white roses all over them. Also, they are completely shapeless. They hang off our shoulders like big flowery sacks. And they have wide scoop necks that plunge halfway down my chest. There will be no leaning over at this wedding, no sir. Not unless I want to give all the guests a terrific shot all the way down my nonexistent chest. I've been practicing standing ramrod straight ever since I first saw the dresses.

"In, in, in!" Esme barks at me. I take the dress and change in a corner while Lucille keeps moaning and poking herself. She is right, I'm afraid. The dress does, um . . . accentuate her bulges. But, to be fair, I'm not sure there's a dress in the world that could hide them.

"Lucille," Vicky finally snaps, "are you my

maid of honor or aren't you? I mean, can I get a little support, please?"

I wish Sofia were in here, so I could whisper, "Actually, I think it's *Lucille* who needs the 'support,' if you know what I mean." Oh, that's terrible. Karma's going to get me just for thinking that.

"I'm just *saying*," Lucille whines, "that I look totally *horrible* in this dress."

"Well, you don't," Vicky barks. "So shut up about it." I swear, Vicky used to be very sweet. In sort of a sugary, look-how-much-nicer-I-am-than-Paris sort of a way, but still. It's only since she got engaged that she's turned into such a harpy. I have to wonder if Kevin is starting to worry about what he's getting himself into.

"Girls, girls," Carolina intervenes. "There is nothing to fight about. Victoria, it's a lovely dress, and Lucille, all you need is some figure-enhancing underwear. Trust me, I can recommend the perfect bustier—my brides use it all the time. It'll make a world of difference."

See? This is why we pay her the big bucks. In

minutes, everything is smoothed over, and Lucille and Victoria are best friends again. Sometimes I wonder what Carolina would do if I started whining, too. Could she magically fix all my problems—like the Wedding Curse? Hmmm. I wonder what her solution would be for the ginormous crush I have on her son. I think I won't be mentioning that.

As Esme fusses around me with pins clamped between her lips, Carolina tries the tiaras on Victoria. When I mention Leo's suggestion about the flowers in her hair, Vicky flips out.

"Oh my God!" she squeals. "That would be PERFECT! That would be SO PERFECT! Carolina, could we do that, really?"

"Of course we can, darling," Carolina says, patting Vicky on the head. "Right, Kathy?"

Mom nods wearily from her spot in the other armchair. This kind of excursion tends to tire her out. I don't know if it's the yelling, the primping, or the full-on attention her daughters demand while they're in the spotlight, but she always has to take a long nap whenever we get home from a wedding-related outing.

"Oh, and Victoria," Carolina says, "I thought perhaps next Sunday we could work on the favors and the place cards. Wouldn't that be fun?"

"Sure," Vicky says. "Sofia probably has to study for finals, but Jack can help us."

Awesome. Another Sunday lost to wedding prep. I do believe I used to have friends and go out on weekends, but that was in the long-distant past. No, I'm kidding; I do still have friends—Rose, Kim, Mark, and Juanita—but as soon as school is over, they're all going off on exciting summer adventures, like working in theme parks and interning at fashion magazines and stuff, while I get to stay here, serving ice cream and being a part of not only one, but two crazy sisters' weddings. Thank goodness Sofia will be home all summer, too, getting ready for grad school in the fall.

"Don't worry, girls," Carolina says. "I'll have my son Leo help us. He's a hard worker—we'll be done in no time."

Hmmmm. Things are looking up. I mean, vow or no vow, I can still enjoy his company, right? How bad could anything be, with handsome scenery like that around?

Maybe this summer won't be so terrible after all.

Chapter Four

Sofia goes back to school on Sunday night, so I'm stuck listening to Mom and Dad and Paris fighting for the rest of the week. As you can imagine, it's a great environment for studying for finals. But at least I have a good excuse to stay in my room and keep my head down. The last thing I want to do is get involved in this argument.

Tuesday night, Paris storms into my room, slams the door, and throws herself dramatically down on the bed.

"My GOD," she announces. "I'm SO GLAD that at least you and Sofia are on my side."

I really don't know how I ended up on Paris's

"side" of anything. I would have considered that impossible by definition, since normally Paris is a side unto herself.

"So what are you doing on Saturday?" Paris demands. "We have to find a place for the wedding."

"Oh—well, actually—"

"I definitely want a beach wedding," she barrels on, "so we should do some research online. Try the Wedding Channel. Or The Knot." She waves imperiously at my computer.

"Right now?"

"Of course right now! We only have three months! There's no time for goofing around, Jack!"

"Well, I sort of have studying to do—there's a paper due on Friday."

"Jack, please," Paris says, sitting up. "There will always be papers due, but *I* am only getting married *once* in your *lifetime*."

Ha. Ask me why I find this hard to believe.

"And you're my *bridesmaid*," Paris wheedles, "and this is my special day. Come on, please

please please? I swear it'll be fun."

It is not fun. Paris decides that I'm not clicking on things fast enough, so she shoves me out of my own chair and monopolizes my computer for the next two hours. There is no need for this, believe me. We have two other computers with Internet access: one in my parents' study and one in the den for family use. I wonder briefly if I can sneak out and use one of them, and whether Paris will even notice if I'm not here, but the first page of my paper is saved on my computer, and there's no way I'll be able to recreate that brilliance again.

Besides, Paris keeps whipping around going, "Oh my GOD! What do you think of this one? Isn't it GORGEOUS?"

Luckily all I have to say is "yeah, wow," and she moves on.

Finally she goes away, and I end up staying up until two A.M. finishing my homework and getting nowhere on my paper. I cannot WAIT for senior year. If this wedding really happens, surely Paris will move out and go live with Jiro. I'm not sure our house will know how to deal with that much peace and quiet.

Speaking of Jiro, for now Paris has sent him back to New York, where he lives with a bunch of other models. But on Thursday at dinner she announces that she wants us to have a family event where we can all meet him.

"I think that will solve everything," she says (dramatically, as usual). "Then you'll see how perfect he is, and you won't want to stand in the way of our love anymore."

Dad rolls his eyes at Mom. Paris doesn't notice, but I do. He does that pretty often, actually, especially when Paris is involved. Dad is kind of a bossyboots, and Paris is the only one of us who ever fights with him like this.

"Come on!" Paris says. "Alex and Sydney and Victoria all got engagement parties!"

"That's because Alex and Sydney and Victoria all had real engagements," Dad says, wagging his fork at her.

"Just a barbecue," Paris whines. "Just family. It's not a big deal. I just want you all to meet him. Would that be so bad?"

Mom reaches over and touches Dad's hand. "Perhaps we should give him a chance, Ken," she says. From this I can tell that she has already caved, at least on the inside, which means Dad giving in is not far behind. This wedding is a go.

"I have nothing against *him*!" Dad protests. "I'm sure he's a lovely young man. I just have a problem with Paris being impetuous and rushing everything, as usual. Why not date him for a year before making any rash decisions?"

Paris takes a deep breath, but Dad cuts her off before she can start bellowing again. "I know, I know, because you *love* him," he grumbles.

"How about Sunday?" Paris says perkily. "We'll have everyone over for burgers."

"Sofia has finals," I point out.

"I'm sure she'll come back for something as important as *this*," Paris says.

"And we're supposed to work on Victoria's favors and place cards," I add.

Paris blows up. "Victoria, Victoria, Victoria!" she yells. "We've been working on her wedding for MONTHS!" This is true. "Why can't we spend ONE SECOND on ME for once? I NEVER ask for ANYTHING!" This is definitely not true.

"All right, sweetie," Mom says soothingly. "Let's do it the following Sunday, so Sofia can be here and we can make the day all about you and Jiro. All right?"

"Fine," Paris says, stabbing her meatloaf.

"Just family," Dad says sternly. "Like you said."

"And Carolina," Paris says. "I mean, she *is* my wedding planner."

"Fine," Dad agrees, and there is nothing I can do to stop myself from hoping that Leo will come as well. What is WRONG with me?

I do manage to get my paper in on time on Friday, but I have another one due on Monday that I haven't even started. And of course, on Saturday, Paris bursts into my room at eight o'clock in the morning.

"Ready?" she squeals, even though I am clearly still huddled under the covers and not "ready" for anything but more sleep. "Come on, rise and shine," she says, poking my shoulder and bouncing on the mattress. "We have a lot of places to see."

"Rrrrrrrrrrrrrrrr," I mumble. "Later. Sleep more."

"No, we have to go," Paris says, bouncing on the mattress again. "I told Carolina we'd pick up her and her assistant at eight thirty, because she has to be back for a meeting with another client at three."

I poke my head out from the blanket. "Assistant?"

"Yeah, her son is working for her this summer or something."

I am out of bed before Paris even finishes her sentence. Half an hour to shower, pick an outfit, and get ready before finding myself in a car with Leo. I'll have to go with my safety outfit: bootcut jeans and a black fitted T-shirt. It's not date-me, date-me hot, but I know it looks good on me, especially with the jade earrings my parents bought for me the last time they were in New Zealand.

I mean, not that I care if I look good for Leo, of course. Since dating him is not an option. But if you're going to be in the company of someone that good-looking, you should at least make a little effort, don't you think? That's all that's going on here.

Paris shoves me into the front seat of her jeep, but when we get to the Trapelos' house, she says, "Okay, get in the back, Jack. Carolina should ride up front so we can talk wedding stuff."

I hop out just as Carolina and Leo emerge from their front door. He's wearing his sunglasses again, with a dark green T-shirt and khakis, and he looks totally yummy, especially when he grins at me.

"Good morning, Jack darling," Carolina says, kissing both my cheeks. "I'm sorry you have to be up so early, but we will try to make this not too painful."

"Yeah," Leo says. "See, I brought doughnuts." He holds up a little white bag and . . . well, color me smitten. Hot AND bearing doughnuts? Talk about an unfair combination. But I will be strong, yes I will.

"Come on!" Paris hollers, honking the horn, which I'm sure the neighbors appreciate at this hour of the morning. "We have a lot to do!"

"Ah," Leo whispers to me as we climb into the backseat, "this must be the infamous 'most crazy sister' that you mentioned."

"Welcome to the monkey house," I murmur back.

Paris is already chattering away to Carolina, handing her piles of printouts with all of her potential locations, their prices, maps, directions, etc. It sounds organized, but in reality it's a giant stack of looseleaf that she has dropped several times, so none of the pages that are related are anywhere near one another in the stack. Carolina calmly begins sorting them as Paris peels out onto the road.

"So?" Leo asks me quietly. "What's it like having two sisters getting married at the same time?"

"It's about two hundred times worse than

dealing with one wedding," I say. "But it's only the first week. I'm sure by week five we'll be up to a thousand times worse."

"This should be fun, though," he says. "Don't you love looking at locations? It's like, this is the foundation of the whole wedding. My mom used to take me with her all the time, and we'd act out the whole procession and where everyone would stand and where the cocktail hour would be and good places for pictures and everything." He grins at me, looking a little abashed. "You think I'm really cool now, don't you?"

Actually, I do.

"Don't you have school or finals right now?" I ask. "How do you have time for this? Because I definitely don't." Yes, okay, I'm fishing. I'm still not sure how old he is, and he can't possibly go to my school, or I'd have noticed him.

"Yeah, finals," he says. "Tell me about it. Plus Mom wants me to start thinking about college applications already."

A clue!

"You're a junior, too?" I ask, surprised.

"Yeah, over at Ben Franklin Academy." That's a private school—no wonder I haven't seen him around. "I can't wait for summer."

"Me too," I agree. "Although it'll be mostly weddings and serving ice cream for me."

"Ice cream?"

"I work at The Yummery in town. Just Monday and Wednesday nights for now, but I'm hoping to fit in more this summer."

"Here's the first place!" Paris trills, pulling into a parking lot. "It's a country club, but not one of the really expensive ones, and supposedly they have a great beach."

"Yes," Carolina says, but I hear a note of doubt in her voice. "Their catering is quite pricey, though."

"Oh, I'm so going to do my own catering," Paris says flippantly. "I make the best fried chicken ever."

Now Carolina looks worried, like she's wondering what she's been dragged into. "Do your own catering, darling?" she says. "That's quite a task to take on."

"It'll be fine," Paris says, turning off the car. "We'll make something really simple, and besides, Sofia and Jack will help me."

I give Leo a significant look and he hides a grin as his mom turns around to check on me.

"Sure," I say politely to Carolina. "I can't wait."

"Well, let's see what we think," Carolina says, climbing out of the car. Leo and I follow more slowly as Paris motors off across the lot and through the front doors.

"Why did you have to come on this excursion?" Leo asks. "Especially if you have finals to study for?"

"Well, I'm the only sister in town that Paris is speaking to," I say wryly. "And Mom is supposed to be finding her dress for Victoria's wedding today. She's been putting it off because she hates shopping. Which, by the way, runs in the family, at least as far as I'm concerned."

"I guess Paris must trust your opinion," he says gallantly, holding the door open for me.

I snort (very elegantly). "You'll see," I say.

Paris and Carolina are already out on the beach with a guy from the country club, who is walking up and down with her, explaining the wedding setup. I perch on the banister of the long stone staircase that leads to the pool and then the beach.

"She doesn't like it," I say.

"How can you tell?" Leo shades his eyes with his hand and squints out at my sister.

"If she did like it, she'd be waving her hands all over the place and nodding a lot. Now she's just kind of frowning and listening. Bad sign."

"You're a keen observer," Leo says.

"Of my sisters?" I reply. "I don't really have a choice. It's either figure out how they think, or get trampled when I don't get out of the way fast enough. I've managed to learn that much in seventeen years." I'm trying to be flippant, but I'm still kind of flattered. I've been thinking lately that I might want to be a journalist, so that sort of compliment is exactly what I want to hear. And it doesn't hurt that he's pushed his sunglasses up on his head and his green eyes are

90

twinkling at me as he says it.

"Wow. I have no idea what that's like," Leo says.

"Only child?" I guess, and he nods. I can't begin to imagine what life would be like if I got all the attention in our house. If I was the only kid Mom and Dad took on vacations. If there were no weddings to deal with until my own.

Of course, if I were an only child, I wouldn't have Sofia. And even Alex, Sydney, Victoria, and Paris are worth it for one Sofia. I mean, I love all my sisters . . . but I love them more when they're not being crazy brides.

Paris comes bounding up the steps, waving her finger in a brisk circle in the air. "Onwards and upwards," she bellows. "Come on, guys."

"Hey, Paris?" I ask as Carolina joins us and we follow her back to the car. "Shouldn't Jiro be here for this? I mean . . . wouldn't he want to see the options too?"

"Pfft," Paris says. "He'll like whatever I like. He's *so* easygoing, you wouldn't believe it. I *love* that."

Plus, I imagine if she dragged Jiro around to all these wedding sites, he might figure out that she thinks they're getting married. I'm still not convinced he knows that's what's happening here.

The next two places are basically wedding factories, with what appears to be the exact same white lattice gazebo planted at the edge of the ocean—"perfect for photographs!" the factory runners coo. Paris latches on to my arm and drags me around behind her, so I don't get to talk to Leo again until the last place. But I can feel him watching me, which makes me feel all weird and tingly inside.

How could he possibly be interested in me? I haven't done anything interesting in front of him. And I'm pretty overshadowed by Paris, who is the very definition of "interesting." Maybe he's just trying to figure out how such a vibrant family ended up with a dud like me.

The last place is Carolina's suggestion. After the second wedding factory, she firmly sets aside Paris's crazy sheaf of ideas and says, "Paris, I know where we should go next."

"Oh, really?" Paris says. "Did you find the map? It's called the Wild Orchid or something like that, isn't it?"

"No," Carolina says. "We're going somewhere else. I think I know the perfect place for you."

"But—" Paris says, reaching for her papers.

"Trust me, darling," Carolina says in a voice that is soothing, yet not to be argued with. I'm starting to think this is going to be an interesting dynamic to watch. If anyone can tame the Paris crazies, it may be Carolina. "Just follow my directions."

I'm really, really surprised when Paris agrees without further argument. She doesn't pipe up again until we pull up to the park ranger's box and pay our two dollars to go inside.

"Carolina," Paris hisses, "this is a national park! I can't get married here!"

"Why not?" Carolina says imperturbably. "Follow the road to the right and park at the end."

I glance at Leo, who is watching me with a

cute grin. Distracting! I stare out the window again as if I am studying our surroundings very carefully.

Tall pine trees line the road, and at the end is a long parking lot in front of a hill of sand dunes. I can tell Paris is still dubious as we climb out of the car, but when we walk up the steps to the top of the hill, suddenly the sun comes bursting out of the clouds and she stops with a gasp.

Spread out before us is a long sandy beach and then the blue-gray sparkling water of the ocean. You can't see any sign of civilization from here, and it looks like a deserted island. It's ridiculously beautiful.

"Oh, Carolina!" Paris shrieks, sort of breaking the moment. "It's perfect! It's SO perfect!" It really is. I feel a pang of regret that Paris got this place first, which means I can't get married here. Not that I'm thinking about that yet, of course. And by the time I get married, like, twenty years from now, everyone will probably have forgotten all the details of my sisters' weddings . . . but still. It seems a bit unfair that Paris should get dibs on such a gorgeous place.

My sister kicks off her slingbacks and races down the hill barefoot toward the water. Carolina looks a bit smug as she follows her.

"Wow," I say to Leo. "Your mom really pegged Paris—and fast."

"She's good," he says. "She's observant, too, like you. You'd probably be really good at her job."

"Oh my LORD," I say. "I could *never* be a wedding planner, are you kidding? I'd totally kill myself."

"Totally?" he jokes. "Not just a little bit kill yourself?"

"I can barely handle four weddings in three years," I say. "And those are people I love— you know, mostly. Imagine dealing with, what, fifteen weddings a year? All of them strangers?"

"More like thirty weddings a year, usually," Leo says.

"I don't know how she does it." I shake my head and sit down to take off my sneakers and socks. Leo does the same, and I notice, unintentionally, that his feet are very nicely shaped—like the rest of him.

"I think you could do it," Leo says. "You just have to care about people and pay attention to them, and you seem to be pretty good at that."

I shove his shoulder, kind of amazed at my own audacity. "You barely even know me."

"Maybe I'm observant, too," he says with that cute grin.

This is getting too flirty for me. We're moving into dangerous territory. I stand up and scramble down the hill in my bare feet. I can hear him following me, but I don't look back.

Paris catches me at the bottom and spins me around with so much excitement that even I start laughing. "Jack, Jack, look how amazing it is!" she crows. "We'll have the ceremony down by the water and then we'll set up a big tent right here for eating and dancing, and it'll be so romantic and perfect, oh my goodness!"

"Not to mention affordable," Carolina adds with a wink. I'm guessing my parents have said something to her—either that they're not paying for it, or that they're only willing to spend a small amount on what they consider to be one of Paris's wild and crazy impulse purchases. One wedding with a side order of husband, please.

The best part of this is that now we can go home, which means I have the whole rest of Saturday for studying. Or so I think.

"Bye, Jack," Leo says in a low (one might even say "sultry") voice as he gets out of the car at the Trapelos'. "See you tomorrow."

Tomorrow! I'd forgotten about the arts and crafts extravaganza for Victoria. I nod and wave as he walks away.

When we get home, I make a dash for the stairs, but Paris seizes my arm and hauls me into the den. "MOOOOOOOM!" she hollers. "DAAAAAAD!"

"Good heavens, Paris," Mom says, coming into the den. "Our office is right there. You don't have to shout."

"We found the most *perfect* place!" Paris announces. "Right, Jack? Isn't it perfect?"

"It's perfect," I agree.

"It's completely amazing and so, so, SO me. Don't you think, Jack? Wasn't it SO me?"

"It is SO her," I agree.

"And everyone is going to totally love it. Right, Jack? Won't everyone totally love it?"

"Everyone will totally love it," I agree.

This goes on for a really, really long time. Finally I escape upstairs to my room with about an hour to study before dinner.

For some reason, though, I'm having trouble focusing on Gabriel García Márquez in Spanish tonight. The words keep blurring on the page, and instead I keep picturing Leo saying "You're a keen observer" with his eyes twinkling. I keep imagining his body next to mine in the backseat, his shoulders and arms and hands only inches away from my own, radiating warmth.

It's probably a bad sign that he manages to distract me this much when he's not even here. I should really put a stop to the flirting. I mean, my choices are: (a) make a move, find out he doesn't like me and is just kidding around, and be horribly humiliated; (b) make a move, find out he likes me, date him, take him to Victoria's wedding, watch the Wedding Curse strike again, destroy the whole wedding, possibly be crushed by falling masonry or whatever disaster strikes next, *and* be horribly humiliated and sad in a whole new way, but this time with a guy I really wouldn't want to lose; or (c) stop everything now, and avoid humiliation (and sadness) (and masonry-crushing) either way.

You might think I'm being dumb, but you didn't see the look on my very first boyfriend's face when I caught Alex's bouquet, or when one of her guests asked him for another slice of cake. And you don't want to know what happened with Boyfriend #2 at Sydney's wedding.

Sorry, Leo. Weddings and relationships just don't mix—at least not for me. Trust me, it's for your own good.

Chapter Five

It shouldn't surprise you to hear that Victoria has decided we will be working on favors starting at eight o'clock on Sunday morning.

"That way we'll be done early," she says enthusiastically. "And then we'll have the rest of the day to get other wedding things done!"

Hooray!

Yeah, I've tried many times to explain to this family that teenagers need more sleep than other age groups. It's true. There was a study or something. We need like nine hours of sleep a night, minimum. And when you're up until two A.M. trying to write a coherent essay about Manifest Destiny while *not* thinking about sparkling green eyes, the last thing you want to see five and a half hours later is your (other) bridezilla sister flitting through your room, throwing up the blinds, and chattering, "Come on, come on! These place cards aren't going to assemble themselves!"

It also shouldn't surprise you to hear that Paris has made herself scarce for the day. She tried to corral me into coming dress shopping with her, but Dad put his foot down and insisted that I was needed here, and that I had to honor my prior commitments. I think he's trying to teach her a lesson, but he really should know by now that that's not going to work.

You know what would be awesome? If one day he would put his foot down and say, "Actually, Jack doesn't have to do any wedding stuff today. Today Jack can go lie around in the sun beside the pool instead."

I am faced with an enormous dilemma when Vicky wakes me at seven thirty. Should I get up, shower, eat a healthy breakfast, and make myself all pretty for when Carolina and Leo get here? Or should I sleep an extra fifteen minutes, roll out of bed, grab a banana, and do the favors in my pajamas?

Given the conclusion I came to last night, it's not that difficult to convince myself to take the extra fifteen minutes of sleep. After all, I am supposed to be driving Leo away, not trying to entice him. Also? Sleeping = awesome.

The doorbell wakes me half an hour later. I bury my head under the pillows. Maybe no one will notice if I don't come out.

Knock knock.

"Go away, Victoria," I mumble.

"But the favors!" says a mock high voice. "The place cards! They neeeed you!"

I sit upright so fast my head spins. Leo is standing in the doorway of my bedroom. He is STANDING IN MY ROOM. There are literally clothes and papers and books covering every inch of floor space between me and him. I can actually see a bra from here, tossed elegantly across a chair. Not to mention *I am still in bed*. In my pajamas, in bed, with my hair all crumpled

102

up around my face instead of pulled back in a neat low ponytail the way I usually wear it. IN BED.

Well. If I was worried about driving him away . . . this ought to do it.

"Ow," I mumble, clutching my head. "What are you *doing* here?"

"Victoria sent me to wake you," he says. I'm pretty sure he's trying not to laugh. He's leaning against the doorframe with a rakish grin on his face. I've changed my mind; he doesn't look like Clive Owen. He looks like that guy Jim from *The Office*, but a little more model-y and with a better wardrobe. I love that guy. Not that I love Leo . . . it's just an observation.

"Look, I know Carolina is practically a part of the family by now," I say, "but strange boys, even ones related to her, are not allowed in my room. I can't believe my dad didn't stop you."

"He's a little preoccupied," Leo says. "There's some kind of origami paper catastrophe. I think your mom is sending him out to get more." He gingerly picks his way across the room, putting his toes down in the few bare pockets of space on the carpet. Much to my horror, he sits down on the bed, facing me.

Now he is really close to me. And as I may have mentioned, I'm wearing my pajamas. We're talking an old T-shirt with large holes in it and a pair of soft black pants. I suppose I should count myself lucky that I'm wearing pants at all. Plus we are on a bed, and he smells like mist and rain forests, and I kind of badly want to grab him and kiss him. Which, of course, is a complete violation of all the decisions I made and rules I set for myself last night. *Do not lean toward him, Jack*, I admonish myself. *Stop staring at his lips. Ack! You're having a meaningful silence! He's staring into your eyes! Break the moment! Break it NOW!*

"It's too early for this," I manage to stammer. I plop my head back on the pillow, where it is farther away from the temptation of his lips. "And you are *way* too chipper, Leo. Don't you need nine hours of sleep too? What is wrong with you?"

"To be fair, I am getting paid," Leo says.

"Mom's giving me twenty bucks an hour to be here—and I think waking you up is probably the least boring way to earn it."

"Maybe you could pay me to get up," I say, trying to unobtrusively comb my hair with my fingers without sitting up. "But I'll warn you, I cost a lot more than twenty bucks." I look at him. "Um, that came out wrong."

"How about I take you out to dinner instead?" he says. He puts his hand down on the mattress on the other side of me and leans on it. Yes. His arms are practically around me, and I'm lying down, and now I am having *really* inappropriate thoughts about his arms and his biceps and his shoulders, and *oh my God, is he leaning toward me?*

"We should go help Victoria," I say, putting my hand on his chest to stop him getting any closer. Except now my hand is on his chest, and it's really well-muscled and . . . distracting.

"How about Wednesday?" he says, smiling. I have to think for a minute before I remember he's talking about the dinner invitation.

"I can't—I have work," I say.

"Okay . . . Thursday?"

"Um, I think we have wedding things to do."

"Like what?"

"We always have wedding things to do," I say. "I mean, so I'll probably always be busy. You know. Two weddings. Busy." My hand is still on his chest, by the way, if you're wondering what happened to the part of my brain that normally is in charge of full sentences.

Now he looks confused, and he moves his hand back, so I do too, regretfully.

"Okay," he says. "I understand." He stands up and starts working his way back to the door. I scramble out of bed.

"But you'll be here next Sunday, right?" I say quickly. Why am I doing this? To be nice. Not to encourage him. No.

He stops in the doorway. "Sunday?"

"For Paris's sort-of engagement party," I say, grabbing a hooded sweatshirt and pulling it on. "She said family plus Carolina, so I think that means you could come, too. She wants us to meet Jiro."

He looks down at his shoes. "Yeah, okay, I could do that." He flashes me the smile again. "Thanks for inviting me."

And then he vanishes out the door before I can clarify that *I* didn't invite him; he *was* invited. Whoops. I hope I didn't send the wrong message there.

I take a few minutes to straighten my hair and pull it back, but I figure the damage is done on the pajama front, so I don't bother to change before joining the others in the living room. The good news: Carolina and Leo brought dough-nuts again. The surprising news: Sydney is here to help, actually acting like a real bridesmaid for once. The bad news (depending on how you look at it): The only spot left is on the floor next to Leo.

I sit down beside him, and he kind of looks at me sideways, still with a puzzled expression on his face.

"All right," Victoria says, clapping her hands together. "We're doing this assembly-line-style, people. I'm all for free expression in my classroom, but in this situation we're going for *my* expression."

"And Kevin's," I add helpfully.

"Yes, yes, whatever," she says, "so the best way to do that is to make sure each one is the same. Jack, do you really think you should be having a doughnut right now? Aren't you worried you'll get sugar all over the place cards?"

"Nope," I say, choosing a Boston creme. "Chocolate, maybe."

"That's not funny," Victoria says.

"Sorry," I say meekly. "I'll be careful."

"Tell us what you want us to do, Victoria," Carolina says smoothly.

Victoria launches into an explanation of her complicated favor idea. First, she will fold the origami paper into a rose. Then Sydney will attach the paper rose to a dark green chopstick with a glittery mini hair clip. Then Mom will carefully place the chopstick inside an ornate little glass vase and fill the vase with enough translucent glass pebbles to keep the chopstick upright. Meanwhile, I will write out the guest's name and table number in my well-practiced wedding handwriting, while Leo keeps track on a list and makes sure I get the table number and the spelling of the name correct. And then Carolina will carefully slide the card inside the vase, around the rose, so you can read the information through the glass.

You may be saying to yourself . . . WHAAAAAT? Why is all this necessary? What's wrong with pre-printed place cards and a cute little mesh bag of Jordan almonds at each seat? I'll tell you what: That's what Alex did.

So, okay, why not something simple like a packet of wildflower seeds and a note that in lieu of fancy favors, a donation has been made to the Pediatric Foundation? Can you guess? Yup: That's what Sydney did.

So Victoria, being an art teacher, simply *had* to come up with something complicated, artsy, elaborate, and, let's face it, as annoying as possible. Oh, but I'd be misleading you if I said we swung right into action on the assembly line.

No, no, no. We can't possibly start before Mom and Victoria review the assigned tables one more time. And then, of course, we have to sit through the huge argument about why the Gallos absolutely could not under any circumstances sit at the same table with the Bransens, and did Great-Aunt Beverly's table have to be so close to the band, and was it really wise to seat Victoria's fellow teachers with her most peculiar (Mom's words, not mine) Renaissance festival friends ("well, they're all SINGLE, *Mom*," Vicky huffs indignantly, as if that means they deserve their punishment).

Suddenly Mom grabs the sheet of paper away from Vicky and squints at it. "Victoria," she says, her voice rising, "have you crossed out two names at this table?"

"Yes," Vicky says, snatching the paper back. "Paris and her guest are not welcome at this wedding anymore."

"Victoria!" Mom says, scandalized. "I understand throwing her out of the wedding party, but she's your *sister*! She *has* to be at your wedding!"

110

"No, she doesn't," Vicky says stubbornly. "I'm not going to hers, and I don't want her at mine. She'll ruin the whole thing if she's there. Just like she always ruins everything."

"But Victoria darling," Carolina points out, "then you'll have two empty seats at your family's table."

"I know," Vicky says, directing a hard stare my way. "I've decided Sofia and Jack will have to bring guests to fill the spaces."

"What?" I protest. "No! Why? That's not fair."

Leo gives me the puzzled look again.

"Just invite someone else," I say quickly. But Vicky is already shaking her head.

"If you two bring guests, it'll be perfect," she says. "Mom and Dad, Alex and Harvey, Sydney and Marco, and then you two with your dates. And you'll all have someone to dance with when the wedding party joins us on the dance floor. Symmetrical and perfect."

"But Paris—" my mom tries to interject.

"Paris Paris Paris!" Vicky snaps. "This is *my*

111

day, and I don't want to hear her name again!"

"This is *my* day" has been Vicky's new favorite phrase for months. Unfortunately, it seems to apply to the entire ten-month engagement period.

"It can't be that hard," Vicky says, poking me with her foot. "Just ask someone. Or I'll do it for you. Oh my God," she says as I open my mouth, "and don't even try to tell me about your stupid Wedding Curse, or so help me I will beat you with one of these vases."

There are lots of things I regret in life, but telling Vicky about my vow is definitely up at the top somewhere. We were commiserating about Sydney's wedding about a year ago, and it was late at night, and I was missing Sofia, and it just spilled out. Luckily I managed not to tell her the whole David story, or I'm sure the entire room would be hearing about that right now, too. And you know, Victoria thought my vow made sense, until *she* got engaged and apparently decided that all the rules would be different for *her* wedding.

"What Wedding Curse?" Leo says alertly.

"Jack thinks if she brings a guy to a wedding, it'll automatically destroy the relationship," Vicky scoffs. "And the wedding."

"Vicky, shut *up*," I say, seizing her foot right before she pokes me with it again. She yanks it away.

"She's decided not to date anyone until after all her sisters' weddings are over, just in case." Vicky rolls her eyes. "Where's your sense of romance, Jack? Weddings are the most romantic things ever."

"Not for boys," I say, "and not for me. Besides, I'm doing this for your own good, Vicky. You're the one whose wedding will be crashed by a motorcycle gang if I bring a date. You should be thanking me."

"But the *love*, and the slow dancing, and the flowers everywhere," Vicky says dreamily. I can see she's not really paying attention to me anymore. She picks up a piece of origami paper and begins to fold it into a rose.

I sneak a glance at Leo. He has an "aha"

expression on his face that I don't like.

"Oh, Jack doesn't have a romantic bone in her body," Sydney says dismissively, taking the rose and attaching it to a chopstick. *I beg your pardon.* This from the girl who wrote her husband's vows *for* him so that she could be sure they'd be short, snappy, easy to say, and acceptable to her. Listen, I am *perfectly* capable of romance with the right guy, but I have no interest in doomed relationships, which is what they would be if they happened during wedding fever season in my family.

"Remember that cute guy Olaf at my wedding?" Sydney goes on. "The one I tried to get you to dance with?"

"The one who looked, talked, drank, and danced like a Viking?" I say. "Yeah, I think my feet still have the bruises."

"He was *cute*," Sydney says. "You could have given him a chance!"

"He was so drunk by the time Sydney brought him over to me, I could smell him coming from across the ballroom," I say to Leo. I do not say that my own date, David, was also pretty drunk by then, a feat he managed without my noticing. "Not to mention he looked like he was about thirty years old."

"See what I mean?" Sydney says. She hands the rose to Mom. "Not one ounce of romance in her." I roll my eyes at Leo, and he grins.

"Not like my Leo," says Carolina, lining up the vases. "He's such a romantic, aren't you, darling?" She pats her son's head, and he looks adorably embarrassed. "I think I exposed him to too many weddings as a child."

How could two weddings have squashed my sense of romance, while a whole lifetime of them has turned him into a true believer?

"So we'll leave those two blank," Leo says, picking up the spreadsheet of table assignments, "and you can figure it out later, right?" He puts a little star in pencil next to where Paris and "Paris's Inevitable Last-Minute Surprise Guest" (that's my dad's sense of humor at work, in case you're wondering) have been crossed off. "Now, what did you decide about the Gallos?"

"Tonya Gallo *hates* Donna Bransen," Mom says. "You *can't* put them together, Victoria."

"But MOOOOOOOM," Victoria whines, "I can't put the Gallos with the Petersons, because Wendy dated Victor in ninth grade and he, like, totally cheated on her and she, like, can barely even forgive me for letting him come to my wedding at all!"

They launch back into that argument, and I give Leo a grateful smile. Did he rescue me from the wedding date/Jack's-not-a-romantic conversation on purpose? I'm pretty sure he did. He smiles back, and my heart flips over a couple of times. Dreamy, observant, gallant . . . *Jack, Jack, Jack, remember the vow!*

But it's awfully hard to keep it in mind while Leo is leaning over me, watching me print out the place cards as neatly as I can, with his arm so close to my arm, and his face so close to my face. . . .

"I think it's supposed to be Tom with an 'm,'" he whispers in my ear.

"I know," I say, jabbing him in the side with my elbow. "Shut up. Stop laughing at me."

Like I said . . . a little distracting.

Chapter Six

I manage to focus on finals for the next couple of days, finishing my paper by Monday and passing a quiz on Tuesday. I'm actually relieved to go to work on Wednesday night, because I know it'll probably be quiet and I can get some work done. It's almost closing time, and I'm leaning on the counter at The Yummery, rereading *The Catcher in the Rye* (two words: yyyyyyy-aaaaaawn), when the little bell tinkles over the door.

"Welcome to The Yummery," I say, stashing the book under the counter. "Can I help you?" I pop back up to find Leo leaning on the counter right across from me. It's probably not the right signal to be sending, but I can't help grinning at him as if he's made of ice cream himself.

"Cute hat," he says. It's this goofy white paper crown with dancing cows in sunglasses on it. You know, to match the cows in sunglasses on the apron I'm also wearing.

"Thanks," I say. "Think Victoria will let me wear it to the wedding?"

"It looks a bit more Paris than Victoria to me," he says. He's quite right about that.

"Tell me about it," I say. "I'm pretty sure I heard her say something on the phone to Jiro last night about overalls. So . . . kill me now, basically."

"You'd be cute in overalls, too," he says. Have I mentioned how nice his shoulders are? They're just the right width and I kind of want to run my hands all over them. I know, I've never thought about shoulder width before either, but he's just so . . . nicely proportioned. And touchable.

"So, what are you doing here?" I ask, veering firmly away from the subject of my cuteness.

"Want some ice cream?"

"Actually," he says, "I'm lactose-intolerant."

I gawp at him. "You mean you can't eat ice cream? Oh my goodness," I say, "what did you do in a former life to deserve that? Were you Jack the Ripper? You were Jack the Ripper, weren't you?"

He laughs. "But I brought you something." He puts a white cardboard box on the counter and slides it over to me. When I open it, I discover that there are seven pieces of different wedding cakes inside.

"WOW," I say, awestruck. "Where'd you get all this cake?"

"My mom had a tasting tonight with a bride who, believe it or not, is not a part of your family."

"Whoa. Those exist?" I joke.

"So I snuck out some of the leftover cake," he says. "I thought you might want to share it with me."

"You're allowed to eat cake?" I ask.

"I can safely try these four," he says, pointing. "Got any forks?"

I produce plastic spoons and glance at the clock. "I think we can close three minutes early tonight. I mean, surely there's no better excuse than cake."

He takes the box to one of the circular booths in the back, out of sight of the window, while I lock the door and finish the last closing-up chores. Finally I slide into the booth across from him.

"Ah," I say, looking at the cake options. "Let me guess—Tammy's Bakery?" He's folded down the edges of the box so we can reach them all.

"Okay, that's impressive," he says.

"Sydney made us visit pretty much every bakery in town," I say. "She wanted something *unusual*."

"Like pineapple upside-down cake?" Leo guesses.

"Like this chocolate and raspberry mousse cake," I say, taking a spoonful of the pink and brown slice.

"That's not so crazy," Leo says.

"I know. But compared to Alex's uber-traditional vanilla pound cake with white but-tercream frosting—like this one here—Sydney thought it was pretty out there. I might have to go with pineapple upside-down cake, though, since my sisters will have used up all the other ideas by the time I get married—you know, in like two hundred years."

"No way," Leo says. "That's only two of the seven choices here. That leaves you at least five excellent options."

"Well, no," I say. "Alex also had a dark chocolate groom's cake like this one. And Victoria is having white chocolate like this one, covered in bazillions of sugar flowers—and real ones, too, I'm sure. I have no idea what Paris will do. Twinkies, maybe, just to be different."

"So that leaves you . . . carrot cake?" Leo says with a grin.

"Oh yay," I say, laughing. "Yeah, I'm afraid that might prove Sydney's theory about how unromantic I am."

He looks down at the cakes again. I don't know why I feel so comfortable with him. He's easy to talk to, and funny, and I feel like he actually understands all this wedding stuff, whereas most of my friends at school have no interest and no idea what I'm talking about when I say things like "fondant" and "tea-length" and "embossed." Believe me, I wish I didn't either. But it's kind of nice to have someone to talk to about it, for once.

We finish the cake samples, talking about which ones we like best and which are too heavy. I'm surprised that we both like the banana-chocolate cake the best—in my family, I'm the only one with a passion for banana-flavored sweets. I'm also a little disappointed that the cakes disappear so fast . . . I mean, I'm quite full of cake, but I wouldn't mind hanging out with Leo a bit longer.

"So," Leo says, taking the last bit of the carrot cake, "is it true? What your sister said about your Wedding Curse theory?"

"It's not a theory," I say, pointing my spoon at him. "It's a scientifically verifiable phenomenon."

"Sounds suspicious," Leo says, following me as I get up and throw out the cardboard box and our spoons. "I mean, I've been to a *lot* of weddings; I think maybe I have a wider database to work from than you do." It really shouldn't be cute when someone says "database," but on him it totally is.

"Not about me, you don't," I say. "You haven't seen the Wedding Curse attack me and smash me to smithereens like it always does." I turn off the light in the back room.

"Smithereens?" he echoes with glee as we walk to the front door.

"It's less funny when it's you," I assure him, turning off the light by the door. Suddenly we're standing in the dark, lit only by the glow of an old-fashioned street light out by the river. The Yummery is in a row of riverside shops, most of which close earlier than we do. I realize that it's getting late; I hope Mom and Dad aren't worried.

I also realize that I'm standing in the dark, alone with the cutest boy in the universe. And he is only a few inches away from me. And my heart is pounding.

"So . . ." he says quietly, "you really don't want to date anyone until after your sisters' weddings?"

I take a deep breath. This is the real test of my vow right here. I'll just explain it to him. It's not him, and it's not that I'm not romantic, but it just wouldn't be a good idea right now. I don't care if he thinks weddings won't scare him, or if he thinks I'm being crazy and superstitious. He hasn't been through a whole wedding with my family yet.

"I just think, if I try, something will go terribly wrong," I say, looking up at him. He has unfairly long eyelashes.

"Well, but you haven't heard my argument," he says.

"Okay," I say, smiling, "tell me your—"

And then he cups his hands around my face, and he kisses me.

Chapter Seven

His lips taste like honey and chocolate (and surprisingly not like carrot cake). Before I can think about what I'm doing, my arms go around his neck, and his hands slide down to my waist. He pulls me closer and kisses me harder, and I kiss him back.

Suddenly a pair of headlights pulls into the parking lot and sweeps over us. I break away from Leo, pressing myself against the wall behind me.

"Uh-oh," I whisper—I'm not sure why, since no one can hear me in here. "I hope that's not my mom. Or my dad. Quick, let's go out and look like we're locking up."

"Or we could hide," he offers cheerfully.

"They'll see the car and break down the door. Or call the cops," I say. "Out!"

I shove him out the door and turn to lock it behind me.

But it's not my mom, or my dad. It's worse. It's Paris.

"Helllllllllooooooo," she says meaningfully, ogling Leo as she gets out of her car. "What have *you* guys been doing?"

"Paris!" I say. "What are you doing here?"

"Mom just realized what time it is and totally freaked out," Paris says. "She sent me to come looking for you. Sooooo . . . whatcha doin'?" She looks Leo up and down.

"I was, um," I stammer. "We were just—"

"I think we have to come clean," Leo says to me. "We might as well confess."

"What?" I squawk.

"Jack wanted my advice about wedding photographers," Leo says. "She was hoping to give you some portfolios at your engagement party and save you some research time." I'm torn between wanting to kiss him again and wanting to kick him in the shins for scaring me like that.

Of course, Paris buys this outrageous lie, because it fits in perfectly with her usual view of the universe revolving around her. "Oh my God!" she shrieks. "That is SO cute! Jack, you are too sweet for words." She throws her arms around me and bounces up and down.

"But honey," she says, pushing me to arm's length again, "you don't have to do that. I have like a bazillion photograper friends. I'm just going to have them take whatever pictures they can at the wedding and that'll be their present to me. I mean, come on, I'm an artist! Of course I know photographers!"

"Oh," I say with wide, innocent eyes. "I guess that was dumb of me."

"Well, I'm glad I caught you before you went to too much trouble," Paris says. "But you know what you *could* research, if you want to help, is where to rent tents and chairs and all that. I just have *no* idea, and I'm *so* busy." She throws her hands up in the air.

"Sure," I say. "I mean, why not, with all my free time." I shoot a look at Leo.

"I can help Jack with that," he says, I think contritely.

"Great!" Paris trills. "Now we'd better get home before Mom has a coronary. Come on, Jack."

She seizes my arm and drags me to my car. I barely have a chance to wave good-bye to Leo, and I don't get to thank him for the cake. Or, you know, the other thing.

As I pull out, under Paris's watchful eye, I can see Leo standing under the streetlight. He waves, and then touches his fingers briefly to his lips. I don't know if he is blowing me a surreptitious kiss, or if he's just remembering what it felt like.

I'm remembering what it felt like. It's as if I can feel his lips still burning against mine. My mouth is tingling and I feel a little dizzy, like maybe he should come with a warning label—"no operating heavy machinery after kissing Leo."

What was I thinking? What happened to my vow?

As amazing as the kiss was, we had very nearly been caught by the worst person possible. It's like the universe was sending me a warning sign: You don't want to go down this path, or there will be TERRIBLE CONSEQUENCES.

I realize when I get home that I've forgotten my copy of *Catcher in the Rye* at The Yummery, but that's okay. I don't think I'd be able to concentrate on reading it tonight anyway, not with visions of Leo still dancing in my head.

I have to tell him we can't do this. There can be no more kissing. Maybe in September, after Paris's wedding . . . but definitely not until then.

I have a few days to prepare myself, since I don't see him again until Sunday. On Saturday morning Victoria demands I help her choose table linens. TABLE LINENS. As if I have ANY OPINIONS about the color of tablecloths. I think she just wants to prove that she can take me away from Paris, because I was her bridesmaid first, and I happen to be the only one available to make this point with.

So I spend the whole morning blearily watching the woman at the botanical gardens manor spreading out tablecloth after tablecloth for Victoria, then pairing them with different colors of napkins.

"What do you think, Jack?" Vicky asks, and I blink, trying to look awake.

"Um . . . I like the lavender," I say, figuring this is a safe bet. Actually I think the royal blue is kind of cool, but it doesn't go with her pastel colors. Victoria wrinkles up her nose as if this is not helpful, so I add, "The lavender and the baby blue look nice together."

"I think I like the pink," Victoria says decisively. "The bright rose pink for the tablecloths and the light pearl pink for the napkins. That's what we'll do."

Fabulous. Glad I could help.

Then in the afternoon Paris throws me in her car and forces me to go grocery shopping with her. She's decided the engagement party (that's what she's calling it; nobody else is) is her opportunity to test out some of her catering ideas for the wedding. I'd point out that cooking for twelve people is quite different from cooking for a hundred, but this, I know full well, will do no good, so I keep quiet as she buys a ton of corn on the cob, potatoes, and chicken.

Sunday there is still no sleep for the weary, as Paris drags me out of bed to mash potatoes and batter chicken with Mom, while Paris flies around the kitchen in a frenzy, doing very little actual cooking, as far as I can tell. Dad is normally our family chef, but he steers clear today, only occasionally drifting by the door with a concerned expression. It seems like they've accepted that they can't stop this wedding; they've even postponed their trip to Costa Rica, which didn't make them or their editors very happy.

I escape the kitchen for an hour to shower and change, so when Carolina and Leo arrive, I am fully presentable, for once.

Leo's eyes go straight to me as they walk in the door. We're trapped in the front hallway for a minute as everyone says hello to one another, but as soon as the others move on, Leo leans down to me and whispers, "I was hoping I'd get to wake you up again . . . maybe in a more exciting way this time." He touches my face with his hand and brushes his thumb across my lips. It sends shivers of happiness all along my skin.

"Stop that," I whisper, stepping back. "I have a vow, remember?"

"But—" he starts.

"I know," I say, holding up one hand. "You presented a very compelling argument. And then we were nearly caught by Paris, which, if you ask me, was a pretty compelling argument for the other side."

"Mine didn't win?" he says, pretending to look injured.

Just then the doorbell rings, and Paris comes racing back into the hall. She throws open the door and flings herself into the arms of the guy standing on the front steps, who, luckily, is Jiro, and not Harvey or Marco.

"You're here!" Paris shrieks. She covers his face with kisses and he looks embarrassed but pleased, smiling and kissing her back while trying to nod politely to the family members gathering in the doorway.

Alex and Harvey pull into the driveway behind them. Man, if anything could make me more tired than I already am, it's the presence of Harvey. His conversations are the world's best cure for insomnia. I can see him talking to Alex as they park, and even she looks a little sleepy.

Right behind them are Sydney and Marco, and a few minutes later, Sofia arrives, so the house is full of chaos. Leo is shepherded off to the yard while I have to join Paris in the kitchen.

"Hey," Sofia says, coming up behind me and giving me an enormous hug. "How's it going?" She is smiling from ear to ear in a strangely glowing way. I tilt my head at her.

"What's going on with you?" I ask. "You seem really happy about something."

"Oh, it's nothing," she says. "I'm just excited about graduation."

I'm pretty sure that's not the whole story, but Paris is right there, so maybe it's something

134

Sofia doesn't want everyone else to know. I'll have to wait and try to weasel it out of her later.

Paris throws platters into our hands and we carry them out to the buffet table on the deck. In addition to her wedding tester menu, Dad has wisely opted to make some hamburgers on the outside grill, "in case anyone doesn't eat chicken," he hedges, but we all know it's more like "in case Paris's food is mildly deadly."

Everyone is surprised when Jiro points to one of the veggie burgers Dad has thrown on for Sydney and Marco, our only two vegetarians. But nobody is more surprised than Paris.

"You don't eat meat?" she says to him.

"No meat," he says shyly.

"That is *so* weird," Paris says. "I can't believe I didn't know that."

Sydney and Alex roll their eyes at each other. Dad looks appalled, and Mom just looks queasy.

But the truth is, Jiro seems really sweet. He helps clear away the dishes (so does Leo, I might add), and he listens to Harvey go on and on (I'm sure it helps that he has no idea what Harvey is saying), and then he agreeably goes to the bottom of the yard to play Frisbee with Marco, Sydney, and Dublin. Mom and Dad try out the Taiwanese they know on him, and he doesn't even correct their pronunciation.

By the end of the afternoon, I for one am wondering what this poor guy ever did to deserve getting saddled with Paris.

Dublin steals the Frisbee from Sydney and Marco, so they come back to the deck for fruit salad. I hop off onto the grass and follow the dog's wagging tail behind a clump of tall bushes at the bottom of our garden at the edge of the woods.

I guess there's a part of me that's hoping Leo will follow me back there . . . and he does.

"Oh, hi," I say, turning around with the Frisbee in my hand. He steps between the trees and glances back to where the deck is hidden by the leaves.

"Hey," he says, taking my free hand. Before I can stop him, he bends down and kisses me again, and that is not a helpful way to make me tell him what I have to tell him.

But I force myself to push him away (eventually . . . okay, I'm not a martyr or anything). "Leo, we really shouldn't," I say. "I like you, I really, really do—you have no idea—but that makes it worse, because I know how awful it's going to be when something goes terribly wrong, which it will. Believe me."

"Nothing's going to go wrong," Leo says, his green eyes serious. "Jack, I've wanted to be with you from the first moment I saw you. If you like me too, why shouldn't we give it a shot?"

Because I'm not like my sisters. I don't rush into things. And it's better not to have you in the first place than to lose you later, when it'll hurt so much more.

I shake my head. "I'm sorry. I've been through this before. It's better this way." I push through the bushes and start walking back up to the deck. After a moment, Leo catches up with me.

"Okay . . . but we can still be friends, right?" Leo says. I'm relieved that he doesn't sound hurt or offended or mad at me. He sounds like he thinks it's no big deal, which is good . . . that's the whole idea, right? To keep things casual, so we can't get hurt? So why do I find myself wishing he were just a little more upset?

"Of course," I agree, smiling to show him everything is fine. "Friends. I mean, we'll be seeing a lot of each other this summer, I think."

"Yeah," he says. "And, um . . . you will let me know if you change your mind, right? About dating?"

"All right," I say. "But don't get your hopes up."

"Yes, ma'am," he says.

We cross the lawn and rejoin the others by the barbecue. As I watch Leo joking with Dad, I think about what it felt like when he kissed me . . . and I hope I'm not making a huge mistake.

Chapter Eight

The following weekend is Sofia's college graduation, not that anyone seems to remember that in all the manic wedding activity going on around our house. But *I* remember, and I've been planning my graduation present for her for months.

What I'd really like to do is take her somewhere for a weekend—away from weddings and sisters and craziness—but I can't afford that, so instead I've been putting together a photo album of her life, starting with baby pictures and going all the way up until her graduation, which I'm saving the last couple of pages for.

The plan was originally for me, Mom, Dad,

Vicky, and Paris to drive up on Saturday and stay in a hotel for the weekend, while Sydney and Alex and their husbands joined us just for the ceremony on Sunday. But now Vicky and Paris are both refusing to either ride in the same car with each other or stay in the same hotel.

And then on Thursday, Vicky finds out that she can't have the particular flowers she wanted on top of her cake because they're, like, poisonous (seriously), so she flips out. That same day, Paris discovers that the white sandals she wore to her prom SIX YEARS AGO no longer fit and moreover have scuff marks on the heels, so she can no longer wear them for her wedding like she'd planned, which sends *her* into a major spiraling meltdown too. I'm sure I'm not the only one who finds her timing suspicious.

When I get home from school on Friday, Paris is upstairs throwing shoeboxes around her room and yelling at Mom, as if it's Mom's fault that Paris's feet got bigger, while Dad is on the phone with Victoria saying something about how absolutely lovely daffodils are. Poor Dad.

But really, that's what he gets for having six girls.

I go straight to my room and pack a backpack. I reluctantly include a couple of textbooks, since my finals start next week, but I'm pretty sure I won't even look at them. I pack the photo album and my camera in a separate bag to keep them safe. Then I go downstairs and shove a note under my dad's nose.

It says:

I'm taking the Toyota and going to stay with Sofia tonight. I'll see you there tomorrow . . . hopefully!

Dad looks at me wearily and nods. He can't even interrupt Victoria's ranting long enough to argue with me or give me a stern lecture about safe driving. From the look on his face, I bet he wishes he could escape with me too.

I hurry out the door and jump in the car before anyone can stop me. It means Mom and Dad will have to get a ride with Paris or Victoria tomorrow, but there is no way I can stay in our house another night . . . and besides, Sofia is more important. She should have at least one member of her family acting like her college graduation is just as important as some wedding.

It doesn't occur to me to call Sofia and tell her I'm coming a night early. After all, I've crashed on her floor at college a million times, and I figure I can help her pack and prepare her for the wedding madness heading her way. Besides, I never use the phone while I'm driving—it's one of Dad's strictest rules.

It doesn't occur to me to warn her as I pull into the visitor parking lot, or as I follow a bunch of hooting seniors through the swipe-card door into her dorm. In fact, it doesn't occur to me at all until I open the door to her room, hear a startled shriek, and see what I am pretty sure is a *naked boy* hurtle himself out of her bed and dash into the bathroom.

"Jack!" Sofia yelps, sitting up with the bedcovers clutched to her chest. "What are you doing here?"

I would say something witty or at least informational, but my jaw has hit the floor and doesn't seem to be coming back anytime soon. I had no idea she was dating anyone. I mean . . . why wouldn't she have told me?

Then Sofia—because she is Sofia and she is wonderful—starts cracking up. Any of my other sisters would be furious if I walked in on them like this, but Sofia just thinks it's hilarious.

"Oh my God, your face," she says, shaking with laughter. "I've never seen you look so horrified."

"Well, good grief, Sofia," I say, trying to smile. "Shouldn't there be a tie on the door or something?"

"I have a single," Sofia reminds me. "And *most* people don't just barge in without knocking. But come in, and shut the door."

"What about poor Mister Mystery Man in the bathroom?" I say.

"Oh—right. Actually, could you wait outside for a minute?"

"Sure." I close the door and sit down in her hallway. I have no idea what to think. The only guy Sofia ever dated was Ben, the one from England, and that was really serious, until his semester abroad was over and he had to go home. She'd told me everything about it while it was happening. He came to a couple of family barbecues, not to mention Sydney's wedding, of course. Why wouldn't she have told me about this new guy?

Finally Sofia opens the door and lets me back into her room. She's fully clothed now, and so is the guy sitting on her bed, looking very sheepish.

My mouth drops open again.

"Jack," Sofia says happily, "you remember Ben."

Yeah, I do. I remember how brokenhearted she was after he left, and how they spent months e-mailing and racking up huge international long-distance bills before agreeing to "see other people."

"Hey, Jack," Ben says in his much-too-cute British accent. "Nice to see you again." He has sandy blond hair and kind of a Heath-Ledger-meets-Merchant-Ivory look about him.

"Um . . . you too?" I say, shooting Sofia a look.

"Okay," she says. "I think I have to take Jack to the snack bar for a milk shake and a quick chat. We'll be back in about half an hour, okay, Ben?"

"No worries," he says. "I'll finish reading your thesis while you're gone."

"Yeah, right," Sofia says with a grin. "The Xbox is in the common room."

"Sweet," he says, jumping to his feet.

Soon Sofia and I are sitting in a booth with two chocolate milk shakes and a plate of cheese fries, which I have demanded because I think cheese fries are the least she can do to make up for not telling me about the Return of Ben for, as it turns out, *three months*.

"Three *months*?" I say.

"He just showed up," Sofia says, tearing the wrapper off her straw. "He appeared, like a vision, outside my window in the middle of the night. He said he's been thinking about me ever since he left and he can't live without me." She pokes her milk shake and sighs dreamily. "I knew it. I knew he was the Love of My Life."

"Okay, Sofia," I say, "this is the very first time I have ever seen evidence that you're related to our other sisters. I mean, you sound like Victoria. Or worse, Paris."

"This is so different!" Sofia says earnestly. "I didn't just meet him, like Paris and Jiro."

"And he's not a total dork, like Kevin," I muse. "That is true."

"Besides, we're not getting married or anything crazy like that," Sofia says. "But he got a job in the States for the summer, so we're going to just kinda . . . see what happens."

"Do *not* bring him to Victoria's wedding," I say, pointing a fry at her. "I am warning you. You will seriously regret it."

"Oh, we'll see," Sofia says, taking a sip of her milk shake. "I mean, if Paris really isn't going, there would be room at our table . . ."

Sigh. This is going to make it harder than ever for me to avoid getting paired up with someone by Victoria. Maybe she'll let me bring one of my friends from school, if I can get them to come back from their thrilling

146

adventures for a weekend.

"So—why didn't you tell me?" I ask.

"I . . . well . . . I don't know," Sofia says. "I mean, a lot of reasons. I didn't know what was going to happen with Ben—he showed up so suddenly, and it did seem kind of crazy jumping back into things. I wasn't sure what anyone would think. And you have your vow, so I kind of felt bad dating when you're not with anyone."

"Sofia, please," I say, "don't ever worry about that again. I want to know what's happening with you, and I'll never judge you. That's my job as best sister . . . to support you no matter what."

She smiles. "I know you do. I'm sorry I didn't tell you."

"Well, now I know why you've been so cheerful lately," I say, snagging two more fries.

"Hey, I'm always cheerful!"

"Yeah, but this is different." I smile at her. "I'm glad you're happy."

"Me too," she says with a goofy grin. She

pauses, watching me dip my fries in ketchup. "Um, so . . . Mom and Dad aren't showing up tonight too, are they?"

"Nope. I bet they wish they could, but both Paris and Victoria are freaking out about wedding stuff, so I fled with their car. They'll get a ride up with them tomorrow." I shake my head. "Probably one in each car, so Paris and Vicky can each have someone to complain to the whole way."

"Poor Mom and Dad," Sofia says.

"Poor Mom and Dad nothin'," I say. "Poor *me*. I'm the one Paris wakes up at three A.M. to ask if I prefer sunflowers or snapdragons. I'm the one Victoria keeps e-mailing to find her the lyrics of all these different songs, so she can pick a first dance. I mean, has the girl seriously not heard of Google? Why is this my job?"

"You should tell them to leave you alone," Sofia says. "Tell them you have finals."

"Sure," I say. "Like you'd ever do that."

"Well, it's not really fair to you, being the one who's been home for all of these weddings,"

Sofia says. "I'm sorry I've been at college for so much of it."

"That's okay." I grin. "You'll make up for it this summer, right?"

"I will!" she says. "I'll start first thing tomorrow."

I steal a large puddle of cheese. "I'm sleeping in the common room tonight, aren't I?"

She makes an anguished face. "Do you mind? It's just—Ben is only here for tonight, because I knew you all were coming tomorrow, so I was kind of hoping to spend some time with him. You know . . . before I'm back living at home and it all gets complicated again."

"It's totally fine," I say. "I should let you enjoy your last couple weeks of happiness, before the Wedding Curse takes you down."

"Not going to happen," Sofia declares. "Okay, let's go back and wrest Ben away from the Xbox. We can all go to dinner together."

"No, no," I say as we stand up. "You two go ahead. I have plenty of studying to do, and you don't need a third wheel on your last night together. I'll just hang out in your common room."

"Oh, Jack," Sofia says, biting her lip. "Are you sure? I feel bad. . . ."

"Don't," I say. "I'll get to hang out with you all summer, and trust me, your common room is *infinitely* preferable to our house right now. I'll be happy just to get some sleep."

Of course, I've forgotten how noisy college kids can be, especially two days before graduation. Luckily Sofia only shares her common room with three other girls, all of them as quiet as she is, or there would probably be people tromping in and out all night long. As it is, I can hear the revelers through the window, hollering and whooping outside late into the night.

At about ten o'clock, I'm hunched over my chemistry textbook, trying to pound formulas into my head, when I hear my cell phone vibrating in the zipper pocket of my backpack. I'm able to dig it out and answer it just before it goes to voice mail, and it isn't until I'm saying hello that I realize I don't recognize the phone number.

"Hello?"

"Hey, Jack."

Oh my goodness. An odd thrill runs through me all the way to my toes as I hear Leo's rumbling voice on my phone. Bad, bad Jack; this is not how I'm supposed to react.

"Leo?" I say. "How did you get my number?"

"Your sister gave it to me," he says.

"Which one?" I ask. "And please don't tell me you're calling about a wedding catastrophe. This is my one night away from wedding catastrophes."

He chuckles, a sweet, friendly sound that makes me want to curl up in his arms. I wrap a blanket around myself and lean back on Sofia's futon.

"Well, yes," he says, "I think Paris was hoping I'd call to harass you about finding those rental equipment places."

I groan woefully. When in the middle of studying for finals was I supposed to do that?

"But," he adds quickly, "I've already done all the research. So you don't have to worry about it."

"Really?" I say. "How is that possible? Are you a superhero? A wedding planning super-hero?"

He laughs again. "I wish I could claim that, but the truth is we have files of all that information in my mom's office. It was pretty easy to pull together."

"Thank goodness," I say. "And thank you so much."

"I figure it was the least I could do after getting you roped into it," Leo says. "And it *is* really the wedding planner's job." He pauses, and I have a feeling we're both thinking about the kiss in the dark.

"So why are you calling?" I ask quickly. "I mean, if it's not to check up on my wedding to-do list?"

"Um . . . just to say hi," he says. "But Paris told me you're hanging out with Sofia, so—"

"Actually, I'm not," I interrupt him. "It turns

out she's got a *boy* here."

"Whoa, really?" he says. "Does Victoria know? Is he going to be her date to the wedding?"

I laugh. "You have been spending too much time with my sisters if that's your first thought."

"You might be right about that," he says. "So tell me about this guy."

It's kind of nice to have someone to talk to about it—someone who hasn't met him and who might be able to be objective because he hasn't been bedazzled by Ben's cute accent. I tell him about how Sofia was totally in love with Ben, and how crushed she was when he left, and how apparently he's been pining for her for the last year. Leo thinks it's sweet, too, so perhaps I'm worrying about nothing, but then again, his mom did say he's a romantic.

I don't tell him the rest of the story about Sydney's wedding, though. I don't tell him about David, and how he dumped me the day after the wedding and admitted he would have done it sooner but he was holding out for, as he put it, "the free food, the open bar, and the awe-some party." I don't tell him the even worse parts of the David story. Or how Sofia and I were lucky to have each other to lean on once Ben and David were gone.

Instead, I change the subject to chemistry and finals, and we commiserate about all the studying we have to do for next week. We talk until almost midnight, and when we hang up, I go straight to sleep, because I want to keep the sound of his voice in my head and dream about the future, when all the weddings will be over and maybe it'll be safe for me to date once again.

Chapter Nine

Victoria and Paris somehow manage not to speak to each other all through Sofia's graduation weekend. There are enough people in our family that they can always find at least one person to force into listening to their wedding woes, even if, sadly, that person is often me. Paris, for instance, talks my ear off for the entire ceremony about how she can't decide what color to dye her hair for her wedding. It's pretty riveting.

But having Sofia home makes a huge difference. Now I can hide in her room to study, and when Paris or Victoria comes looking for me, Sofia can step in to deflect their attention to her.

With her help, I finish all my papers, study for all my finals, and pass with decent enough grades to probably get me into the colleges I want next year.

Finally, June arrives and school ends. We have one week to go until the (first) wedding, and Vicky is totally freaking out. She shows up on our doorstep on Saturday morning (early, of course) and shrieks "SPA DAY!" when I answer the door.

"Vicky," I mumble, rubbing my eyes, "why didn't you just let yourself in?"

"Because I wanted you to get up and answer the door," she says, as if this makes perfect sense. "I've come to abduct you and Sofia for a special bridesmaids spa day. It's my present to you guys! Isn't that exciting? Lucille and Kelly are in the car already."

I peer around her at the two faces pressed against the window of the car. I would pretty much rather do anything in the world than get in the car with these people and be dragged to a spa. I would rather sleep all day. I would rather scoop ice cream for screaming four-year-olds. Heck, I would rather get eaten by polar bears.

For one thing, I don't like spas. I didn't have a great spa experience with the last two weddings. Pedicures I can handle; anything else makes me nervous. I got a massage at Sydney's "special spa bridal shower" day, and it made me feel all greasy and sore afterwards.

Not to mention, spending the day with Victoria and Lucille right now sounds just about the opposite of relaxing. They've been squabbling nonstop over all kinds of stupid bridesmaid stuff. I think Vicky would happily throw her out of the bridal party too, except that she can't decide who would be maid of honor in her place.

But I don't really have a choice, since I've been forbidden to work at The Yummery on weekends during the summer just in case of wedding emergencies, so I go and wake up Sofia, get dressed, and follow her out to Vicky's car.

"Jackie!" Lucille squeals at me. "You are so

cute! Are you so excited about the spa? Have you ever been to a spa?" She says all this in a singsong baby-talk voice.

"I have, yeah," I say, since that seems like the safest answer.

"All right, you guys," Vicky says, handing us each a pamphlet for the spa we're going to. "I've picked a service for each of you and marked it on these pamphlets, so you'll know what you're getting. I think you'll really like them!"

I notice that she's made sure to pick "services" that are all under $45 . . . and that my initials are down next to "facial."

"Um, Vicky?" I say. "I don't really want a facial."

"Sure you do," she trills. "You'll love it."

"I'm okay with my face the way it is," I say. This is about as true for me as it is for any girl I know—some days I hate my skin, some days it's acceptable. I just don't like touching my face, and I certainly don't like anyone else touching it (with, you know, the notable exception of Leo, but that's in a prelude-to-a-kiss kind of way,

158

which is totally different, and was only once, and isn't going to happen again, so . . . yes).

"Facials are *divine*," Lucille gushes. "And you could really use one, honey."

Gee, thanks. "Can't I just get a pedicure?" I say to Vicky.

"I could trade with her," Sofia offers. I see that she's been assigned to a pedicure.

"No," Victoria snaps. "I put a lot of *thought* and *effort* into these decisions, and we're not changing them, and that's final, because this is *my* day."

Sofia pats my arm comfortingly, as if to say, *Don't worry, it'll all be over in a week.* Except it won't, of course, because then there's Paris's wedding to worry about, and if sweet Victoria has been this transformed by the experience, goodness only knows what'll happen to the Tyrant Queen of Crazy.

At the spa, we are each sent off to different areas. I am apparently the only victim of the facial plan, so I am left in a small pink-and-beige waiting room with faint Indian-sounding music playing in the background. After a few moments, a very large blond woman with enormous, muscular arms and severely plucked eyebrows appears from a back room.

"Hello," she says. "I am HELGA!" She seizes my hand in a viselike grip that really should have sent me running for the hills, leaving nothing but a Jack-shaped hole in the wall.

Instead I say, "Nice to meet you, Helga," and try not to wince as she pumps my arm up and down.

"No!" she cries. "It is HELGA!" As far as I can tell, the only difference between what I said and what she said is volume, but I'm not about to shout at her, so I bob my head agreeably.

"This way!" she says, jabbing her finger down the hall. I follow her into a dark, cool, gray room with the same Indian music and the smell of incense, plus a sound machine of bubbling noises that instantly makes me need to pee.

HELGA! shoves a bundle of cloth into my arms.

"Undress," she snaps. "Put on smock. Lie down."

It sounds straightforward enough. But as soon as she slams the door behind her, I get confused. Undress? How much? Surely I don't have to take off everything? I'm here for a facial . . . please tell me I can at least keep my pants on.

I settle on a compromise. Shorts: on. Shirt: off. Bra: on. If I do it wrong and HELGA! yells at me, I'd rather not be scolded naked. Some clothes are better than no clothes. I lie down on the table and pull the sheet over me.

Apparently this is an acceptable decision, because when HELGA! returns she doesn't yell at me. Instead she seizes my hands and shoves them into a pair of heated mittens filled with some kind of paraffin wax or moisturizing something-or-other. It actually feels kind of cool, and I start to think maybe this won't be so bad.

HELGA! applies mysterious things to my face, washing them off with a warm washcloth when she's done. Then she points a large machine at me and flicks a switch. Immediately a hot mist starts wafting around my head.

"Now you are steamed," HELGA! says. "Ten minutes. No moving!"

Of course, the minute she leaves the room, my nose starts to itch. My hands are still trapped in heat wraps under the blanket. *I* am trapped under the blanket. There's no way to get anything to my nose or my nose to anything.

Itch, itch, itch.

Yeah. It's very relaxing.

I try to take my mind off the itching by thinking about something else, but the only thing that springs to mind is Leo, which is very bad. I haven't seen him in two weeks because he's been away helping his mom with a couple of weddings in the mountains, and I've been studying for finals. But we have talked on the phone . . . probably more than we should, because every time I think about him, I think about kissing him, and I really need to make it through the next week without giving in to that impulse.

The door opens and HELGA! comes back in.

Wow . . . thinking about Leo really did manage to take my mind off the itching. HELGA! flicks on a bright light and leans in to inspect my face carefully.

"Hmm," she says. "Much to do! Very bad!"

"Really?" I say weakly. "Maybe we shouldn't mess with it."

"Time to unclog!" she bellows. "Much better then!"

Suddenly she attacks my face with enthusiastic vigor.

"OW!" I shout immediately. What is she *doing*? It feels like she's excavating for diamonds in my skin. With a pair of knives. Dude, nobody told me this would *hurt*.

"Lie still!" she commands.

"Are you sure you're doing this right?" I ask, struggling to my elbows. She doesn't like that very much. She seizes my shoulders and shoves me down flat again.

"LIE STILL," she hollers.

I think, *All right, maybe it's just the first one that hurts. Maybe that was a particularly difficult . . .*

whatever the heck she just yanked out from under my epidermis.

"OW!" I scream again. That one hurt even MORE, which I wouldn't have thought was possible. I'm not standing for this. I don't need to suffer this much for Victoria. It's her wedding, not mine. Nobody's going to be looking at *my* pores. They can just stay clogged, fine by me.

A brief wrestling match ensues. I am determined to get off the table; HELGA! is equally determined to keep me on.

"My pores are fine!" I yell. "All done! Great work! I love it! Let me go!"

"You are terrible client!" she shouts. "Much unclogging still to do!"

Perhaps it will not surprise you to hear that the gigantic Swedish woman with arms the size of small Labradors wins the tussle with the girl whose favorite athletic activity is racing her sisters to the fridge for the last pint of ice cream.

I have no choice but to lie there as she pokes and prods and basically turns my face inside out, and then applies some kind of stinging substance that makes every cell in my face feel like it's on fire.

"So . . . OW," I say. "This really—OW—really hurts—OW."

"Pain is good!" HELGA! insists. "It would not hurt so much if your pores not so bad!"

Well, at least I know all this suffering is my fault, then.

HELGA! smears something all over my face that feels like mud, then waits for it to dry so she can peel it off again. I'm thinking this can't possibly go on much longer, and I let myself fantasize about Leo because anything that'll take my mind off the pain is okay at this point.

Finally, HELGA! peels off the mask, spritzes my face with something light and chemical-smelling, and then smears moisturizer all over my skin.

"Good," she says approvingly. "Much better." She washes off her hands as I lie there wondering whether I now have giant craters in my skin, because that's what it feels like. Then HELGA! switches on the overhead light and leaves to let me dress myself again.

I pull on my shirt and shoes and hobble weakly back out to the waiting room, where she is lying in wait for me. Victoria has kindly informed us that we have to cover the tipping ourselves, so not only did I have to let this madwoman dig through my face, now I have to pay her for it. I hand her a few dollars.

"Thanks very much," I say, and take a deep breath. "HELGA!"

To my immense shock, she cracks a smile.

"Good lungs," she says, whacking me on the back. "Terrible pores, but good lungs!" And she strolls off back to her evil lair. Yeah, I totally don't mean *strolls*. I mean *lumbers*.

In the main waiting room, I find a mirror and discover that now there are bright red spots all over my face. Leo is supposed to see me like this? Over my dead skin cells. Maybe I can steal Alex's veil. And wear it for the rest of my life.

"Don't you feel refreshed?" Lucille proclaims, drifting into the waiting room with Kelly and Victoria. They've all had massages, and the oil is all through their hair, but they do look more relaxed—even Victoria. I guess some people are just spa people, and some people aren't. Me, I'd like to go home and bury my head under my pillows for the rest of the summer.

But much to my horror, Leo is sitting on our front steps when we pull into the driveway. I see Victoria's shoulders tense when she spots him.

"Is something wrong with the wedding?" she shrieks, hurling herself out of the car the minute it's parked. "Is it the band? It's the clarinet player, isn't it? Did he flake out? I always thought he looked suspicious. I'm going to *kill* him!"

"It's not the clarinet player," Leo says, looking amused. "My mom just wanted me to drop off the list of songs the band can play, so you can go over it and pick the ones you like or don't like."

"Oh my lord, if they can't play 'Greensleeves' as I'm walking down the aisle, I will DIE, I will just DIE," Victoria declares, sweeping past him. "Come on, bridesmaids! We've relaxed enough for one day! We have work to do!"

"Yeah," Sofia whispers to me as Lucille and Kelly throw themselves out of the car and chase her inside. "Stop slacking, Jack."

"I'd be happy to work," I whisper back, slowly getting out of the car. "*Please* give me work; just don't make me 'relax' anymore."

Sofia's cell phone rings and her face lights up as she looks at the number. *Ben*, she mouths, then scoots off around the side of the house to talk to him in private.

Leo is still sitting on the porch, waiting for me. I throw my sweatshirt over my head and approach with just my eyes showing, so I can see the ground. "Do NOT look at me," I say as I get closer. "I'm totally hideous right now."

"I highly doubt that," Leo says, with maximum adorableness. He scoots over so I can sit next to him. I swat his hand away when he tries to peek under the sweatshirt. Through the gap I have left for my eyes, I can't help but notice his remarkably well-formed legs, since he is wearing khaki shorts, and his legs are very close to mine on the porch steps. If I leaned just a little

168

to the right, our knees would be touching. Our skin would be touching. I suddenly have a vivid mental image of my bare skin touching his all the way along our bodies, and I have to yank my imagination back from that precipice.

"Seriously," I say, hoping my voice sounds casual enough that he won't guess what just went through my mind. "I used to think the worst thing my sisters could do to me was make me wear a terrible dress. Maybe force me into a terrible hairdo—did I tell you about the one Alex insisted on? She wanted us all to have our hair pulled straight back into these really tight, small buns so we looked like we had practically no hair, basically. On the plus side, it stretched my face so tight I looked like I was kind of grimace-smiling all night long, which at least kept me awake through Harvey's incredibly long, boring speeches."

"Lawyers," Leo says sympathetically. "I've been to a couple of those weddings."

"But I had no idea my sisters could actually permanently disfigure me," I say. "I mean, I think I might be scarred for life."

"No way," he says, touching my knee. His hand is cool against my hot skin, and I nearly miss what he says next, I'm so distracted by the feeling. "No matter what happened, I promise you it's fixable. We're experts at this stuff."

"All right," I say. "Tell me what you'd do for a facial gone horribly awry."

"Ah," he says. "Don't worry, the redness should go down by tomorrow."

I lean over and rest my head on my knees, wrapping my arms around my legs. Under the sweatshirt it's dark and warm, and I feel like I could go to sleep right here, except that Leo's presence beside me has my heart beating too fast for that. After a moment, I feel his hand on my back—hesitantly at first, and then gently rubbing my shoulders. That should definitely keep me awake.

"Haven't you had a facial before?" he asks.

"Nope," I murmur. "Why, have you?"

He laughs. "I've never been *in* a wedding,"

he admits. "I've just stood around the edges of lots of them."

"I didn't want a facial," I say. "I tried to tell her that, but Vicky was all excited about this being her bridesmaid present to us."

"You could have said no," Leo suggests.

"And ruin her special day? I wouldn't dream of it. She's having enough problems with Lucille. I try to be an agreeable bridesmaid."

"That's very thoughtful," Leo says. "I've met plenty of disagreeable bridesmaids, and they do seem to make the whole day harder for the bride."

"Exactly. I just want Victoria to be happy. And for it all to be over," I add with a laugh. His hand moves up my back, under the sweatshirt draped over my head, and he starts stroking my hair. It's the most amazing feeling. See, if a spa were more like this, maybe I could handle it. Although it probably wouldn't be good business practice to have "hot guy lovingly strokes your hair" be one of the services offered. Nor would I like it if it were anyone but Leo doing this, of course.

"Well, they may not show that they appreciate it," Leo says, "but I'm sure they do. You're a kind bridesmaid, and a great sister."

"JAAAAAAACK!" Victoria screams from inside the house. "What are you DOING? WE NEED YOU IN HERE RIGHT NOW!"

I sigh. Leo wraps his arm around my shoulders and squeezes gently. "You'll make it," he says. "Hang in there."

"Thanks, Leo," I say. "You'd make a great bridesmaid yourself." I peek at him through the gap in the sweatshirt and he grins at me before getting up and strolling back to his car.

Inside, Victoria has commandeered my computer because it's the one with iTunes and the best sound. Lucille and Kelly are sprawled across my bed (um, in what universe is that okay?), Mom and Dad have dragged in armchairs, and Sofia has somehow cleared a space for herself on the floor. You know, I love that my parents don't make me clean my room, but I'd also appreciate a little warning before any seven-person gatherings descend on the place.

I join Sofia on the floor as Vicky clicks on a song.

"We're listening to samples of all the songs the band can play," Sofia explains to me. "So Vicky can choose which ones she wants them to do at the wedding."

"'My Heart Will Go On'!" Lucille screeches with delight. "They HAVE to play that! That is the BEST song!"

"Oh, totally!" Vicky agrees, putting a star next to the song name. "I love Celine Dion!"

Sofia starts to giggle. This is because last night I jokingly wrote out a list of the songs that I knew Victoria would pick, because (a) they are played at Every. Single. Wedding. Ever., (b) they are terrible songs that no one can dance to, and (c) I totally hate them, so they're guaranteed to be played at all of my sisters' weddings (except Sofia's, as she has impeccable taste, of course). "My Heart Will Go On" was at the top of the list.

Vicky does, in fact, pick nearly all of them, but it takes a large portion of the day. It isn't until that evening, when I go out the front door to walk Dublin, that I find a small package on the front porch with my name on it. Inside is a face cream with a note from Leo: IT'S IMPOSSIBLE TO MAKE YOU PRETTIER THAN YOU ARE, BUT HOPEFULLY THIS'LL MAKE YOU FEEL BETTER.

It's cool and soothing and smells like coconut, and it really does make my skin feel better, finally.

I send him a short e-mail: MY HERO.

And I go to bed smiling.

Chapter Ten

"EEEEEEEEEEEEEEEEEEEEEEEEEEEE!!!!!!!!!!!!!!!! MY EYES! LOOK AT MY EYES!"

Yes, it's the beautiful bride on her wedding morning. This is how I was woken up the last two times, too. Alexandria woke up with a zit on her forehead ("EEEEEEEEEEEEEEEE-EEEEEEEEEEEE!!!!!!!!! MY FACE! LOOK AT MY FACE!") and Sydney decided on her wedding morning that she had somehow gained twenty pounds overnight (perhaps at the rehearsal dinner) and that her dress was definitely not going to fit.

Victoria is here because she didn't want Kevin to see her before the ceremony, so she slept over at our place the night before. This created a great deal of awkwardness about what to do with Paris, since the two of them *still* haven't spoken to each other since the fight at Victoria's bridal shower. But luckily Paris decided to jet off for the weekend with Jiro to buy their wedding rings from a jewelry designer she knows in Florida. So at least it's not as completely insane around here as it could be.

Sofia opens my door, darts inside with Dublin, and closes it quickly behind her, pressing her back against the door as if she's being chased by werewolves. Our dog gallops over and leaps on the bed with me. He looks nervous, too, burying his face under the pillow next to mine.

"Hair and makeup appointments in an hour," Sofia gasps. "And we'd better get Carolina over here. Victoria didn't sleep well, so her eyes are bloodshot and puffy and she's decided that she can't possibly get married today."

"She wouldn't be one of our sisters if she didn't," I say, sticking my hand out of the covers and feeling around for the phone. Carolina answers after one ring.

"I'm on my way," she says before I can say anything. "Can I bring anything?"

"Doughnuts," I say, and I also explain about Vicky's freak-out.

"No problem," Carolina says. "Be there soon." She hangs up, and I roll myself reluctantly out of bed.

"So Ben is definitely coming," Sofia says nervously. She finally told the rest of the family about him a couple of weeks ago. Vicky couldn't have cared less who he was; she was just thrilled that Sofia found a date to her wedding. As for *my* missing date . . . she hasn't brought it up in a few weeks. I'm hoping she stuck another relative in there, or better yet, left it empty, so I don't have to worry about it. I haven't brought it up because if she's forgotten about it, I certainly don't want to be the one to remind her.

"I'd say that's great," I say, pulling clothes out of drawers, "but you know what I think. Watch out for the curse."

"It's going to be fine," she says. "What could happen?" This makes us both laugh.

"At least you know he loves you," I say. "He's not like David. At least he's said it."

"Most guys aren't like David," Sofia says. "You should give them a chance . . . well, at least one of them." She winks. I've told her about Leo, but I've given her strict instructions to keep me away from him as much as possible.

"After Paris's wedding," I say firmly. "Maybe. Don't forget to wear a button-down shirt for the hair and makeup."

"Please," she says, "like I don't know that. I was in the last two weddings, too!"

As soon as I'm showered and dressed, I join Mom, Carolina, and Sofia as we try to calm Victoria down. Vicky absolutely refuses to eat anything, so Sofia and I split her doughnut between us. Carolina has brought stuff for Vicky's eyes that reduces the puffiness, and by the time her makeup is on and her hair is done, several hours later, my sister looks beautiful, which I tell her.

"Do you really think so?" she says, studying herself in the mirror. We are at the manor in the botanical gardens, in the dressing room. Sydney and Alexandria have been sent to supervise the ceremony setup, Mom is double-checking the centerpieces and table settings, and Sofia is on a mission to get new stockings for the bridesmaids, because Victoria decided at the last minute that the ones we'd already bought were too dark.

"Absolutely," I say, tucking a strand of hair behind the flower crown. "Kevin has no idea how lucky he is." Why *anyone* would marry him, let alone someone as sweet and gorgeous and creative as Vicky, is beyond me, but of course I don't say that.

She smiles. "Oh, I'm pretty lucky, too." She shivers happily. "I'm so excited about marrying him." I like hearing that. As long as Vicky is happy, I don't have to like him, too.

Vicky catches my hand, beaming, and for a moment I catch a glimpse of the sister I liked before she turned into a crazy bride. For a moment she looks sweet and starry-eyed, more excited about being in love than insane about planning a wedding. "Jack," she says, "it's been too busy to really say anything, but I want you to know how much I've appreciated your help with all this."

"Seriously?" I say.

"You think I didn't notice?" she jokes. Um, *yeah*. "It's nice to have someone to rely on," she goes on, turning back to the mirror and fiddling with her hair. "And you're always there for us. So, you know, thanks."

Awww. Man, I am such a sucker for that kind of thing. Alex and Sydney didn't say anything like thank you, but maybe I was less helpful when I was fourteen and fifteen. Or maybe Vicky's just a better sister. I wrap my arms around her shoulders and hug her.

"CAREFUL!" she shrieks. "The HAIR!" I leap back and she wrinkles her nose at me, which makes me start giggling. It'll be great when this wedding is over and Victoria becomes pleasant to spend time with again.

Carolina bustles in with a box that's overflowing with flowers. Right behind her is Leo.

"I beg your pardon," I say. "This is a *girls'* dressing room, young man."

He grins. "I just brought over the bouquets from the florist," he says.

Victoria whirls around and looks him up and down. "I hope you're not wearing that to the wedding," she says to him.

"No, I'm on my way home to change," he says.

"To the wedding?" I ask. "He's coming to the wedding?"

"He's your date," Victoria announces, patting my head patronizingly. "Since you didn't get one for yourself, I found one for you." All my warm fuzzy feelings for her evaporate with remarkable speed. She leans in and whispers, "I'm sure you've never noticed him, but he's actually quite cute."

Yeah. I've never noticed that.

"When did this happen?" I ask, putting my hands on my hips and glaring at him. He lifts his hands with an adorable, "What could I do?" expression as Carolina sets the box of bouquets on the table beside me.

"A few days ago," Vicky says dismissively.

I'm trying to give Leo a severe, disapproving look, but the effect is ruined somewhat by the fact that I start sneezing my head off.

A-choo. A-choo! AAAA-CHOO!

"Uh-oh," Carolina says.

"You should have—*achoo!*—told me," I say to Victoria.

"Jack," she says with a frown, but I can't talk anymore, because my eyes are streaming, my nose is itching, and I'm bent over trying to contain another sneeze.

"This is not so good," Carolina says.

"What is *wrong* with her?" Victoria asks, her voice going up several notches toward hysterical.

"Allergies," Carolina guesses, whisking the box of flowers away from me. I take a deep breath and let out another explosive sneeze.

"She can*not* do that all through my wedding," Victoria says.

I hope it has not escaped your attention, by the way, that the minute I got a date to Victoria's wedding, disaster struck. Coincidence? I think not.

"We'll fix it," Carolina says. "Don't panic, Victoria."

I sneeze so hard I knock myself over.

"I'll take her outside," Leo says, looking concerned. He puts his hand gently on my elbow, tugs me to my feet, and leads me out through the manor to a secluded part of the garden.

"Wow," I say, sinking down on a bench and pressing Kleenex to my face. "I bet I look really glamorous now."

"You always look glamorous," Leo says, sitting down next to me.

"My makeup must be running all over the place."

"Psh," he says. "You don't need makeup."

"This has never happened before," I say. "I mean, at the other two weddings. I get allergies in the spring sometimes, but not like this."

"It's probably the hyacinths," Leo says. "And bad news—they're in the centerpieces, too."

"Of course." I lean my head on his shoulder, trying to breathe properly. He puts his arm around my waist and we sit like that for a moment. Suddenly he snaps his fingers.

"I know what we can do," he says, jumping to his feet. "Don't go near the bouquets, and I'll be right back."

He dashes down the path to the parking lot. I sit there for a minute, patting my face, but it makes me anxious not to be helping with wedding preparations, so I eventually get up and go back into the dressing room.

Victoria is standing in the center of the room with Mom and Alex pulling on her dress and buttoning it. The bouquets are nowhere to be seen, so I guess Carolina has taken them away somewhere. "Are you done sneezing?" Victoria snaps at me. "Oh my God, Mom, *look* at her face. She's totally *ruined* her makeup." As if this is a diabolical scheme I've been planning for months.

"Oh, sweetie," Mom says with a sympathetic look.

"Wow, Jack, you're kind of a mess," Alex says.

"Thanks," I say.

"Well, get dressed!" Victoria orders. "We have to be ready for pictures soon."

I slip into my hideous flower sack as Sofia and Sydney pile in and put on their dresses, too. Our shoes are these grotesque pink sandals that match the color of the roses with green bows on the heels. Victoria was *so* excited when she found them.

"Yikes. What happened to you?" Sofia whispers.

I give her the short version, and she offers to fix my makeup as much as she can in the fifteen minutes before the photographer arrives. As terrible as I look, I must admit I'm grateful that we're doing the photography before the wedding this time. Alex and Sydney both decided to have the photos taken during the cocktail hour at their weddings, which meant we basically missed all the hors d'oeuvres and half the party, it felt like.

"Okay," Victoria says. "Now, we have to hold our bouquets for the photos, so Jack, do you think you can contain yourself this time?"

"I'm not doing it on purpose," I say.

"Just hold your breath or something," Vicky says. "Come on, everyone."

We follow her out to the gazebo, where Lucille and Kelly are already waiting for us. Carolina is there, too, holding the box of bouquets and looking concerned. As we get closer, I can already feel my eyes and nose reacting, and even my throat starts to close up a bit.

"Ruh-roh," I whisper to Sofia, pulling out my Kleenex again.

Then suddenly, like a superhero sweeping in from the sky, Leo comes racing down from the parking lot. His arms are piled high with hyacinths, which is puzzling, to say the least. I've never heard of treating allergies with even MORE of the offending item.

"Here," he says, gasping, as he reaches his

mom. "Replace them with these." He takes one of the bouquets and carefully removes the hyacinths. With deft fingers, he shoves the stems of the new flowers into the ribbon instead. Then he rearranges it a little to look nice again and brings it over to me.

"What do you think?" he says. I take the bouquet and realize that the new flowers are not real—they're made of silk. But from afar they look exactly the same as the old ones. I beam at him.

"You're a superstar," I say.

Victoria peers over my shoulder at the bouquet.

"Silk flowers?" she cries. "Isn't that kind of tacky? I want only *real* flowers at my wedding!"

"Victoria," Carolina says firmly, "either you accept the silk flowers, or Jack won't be able to breathe for your entire wedding."

Vicky actually hesitates, and I get the strong impression that my personal suffering is not being included in this particular calculation.

"Vicky, you can't even tell they're silk," Sofia

says. "And this means they won't wilt. And they're really pretty."

"I suppose," Vicky relents. "But hurry, we need to do the pictures."

Carolina and Leo work fast, switching out the flowers in all the bouquets and handing them to each of us. There are a truckload of bridesmaids here, but they finish quickly. Then they run off to change out the flowers in the centerpieces too.

Leo catches my hand before he goes. "See?" he whispers, pulling me to the side. "Disaster averted. Maybe we beat the curse, huh?"

I can't help but smile. "That was pretty amazing," I admit.

"So you'll forgive me for being your surprise date?" he says, his green eyes sparkling.

"After this?" I say. "I'd forgive you for being my surprise serial killer."

He grins, glances over at the flurry of bridesmaids who are paying no attention to us, and then kisses me quickly on the lips. I can still feel the warmth of his mouth and the feel of his hand in mine as I watch him run off after Carolina.

The ceremony is a little bit painful, especially in those shoes, which Victoria absolutely forbade us to break in because she wanted them to look perfectly perfect, so none of us have even worn them before. We stand there, trying not to fidget, as the minister drones on for a whole HOUR, interspersed with Victoria's friends reading Shakespeare sonnets and epic medieval poetry and goodness knows what else they're going on about, except that it seems to involve the words "thee" and "thou" a lot.

It's an enormous relief to get to the cocktail hour, and it doesn't hurt that Leo is there waiting for me, looking shockingly gorgeous in a dark gray suit and a lavender silk tie.

"Hey," I say, feeling weirdly shy all of a sudden. How am I supposed to act with a guy Victoria set me up with, but whom I would happily date in *any* other situation but this one? "You look . . . really great."

189

"Thanks," he says, sounding genuinely pleased. "You look great, too."

This makes me laugh, which breaks the tension. "You big liar," I say, shoving him. "No one could possibly look great in this dress—not even Sydney, my super-fit sister, or Sofia, my super-beautiful sister."

"I think you're the super-beautiful sister," he says.

Luckily I don't have to respond to this because a waiter pops up between us with a tray of bacon-wrapped scallops, and then Sofia and Ben join us. Sofia introduces Ben to Leo, and they shake hands.

"I'm glad Jack will have someone to dance with," Sofia says. "Just don't do anything to cement her Wedding Curse theory, mister." She sounds like she's joking, but I know that if he treats me the way David did, he'll have one angry sister to deal with.

Leo laughs and crosses his heart. "I promise."

"Oooh," I say, "I think those are the California rolls going by over there."

"Allow me," Leo says, and dashes off to grab some for us.

"So," Sofia says meaningfully, "you're having fun, aren't you?"

"I'm pretty much holding my breath," I say, "hoping the allergic reaction was the worst thing that'll happen. Keeping a watchful eye on the sky, though."

"Just relax and enjoy it," she says as Leo returns, triumphant.

Several tiny appetizers later, we are allowed onto the wide terrace where the reception is. Leo gallantly escorts me to our table and we all stand as the band leader introduces "for the first time ever, Mr. and Mrs. Kevin Ork!"

"Yikes," I say, clapping along with everyone else.

"I've always found that weird," Leo says. "I mean, it's like her own name completely disappears."

"Exactly! It weirded me out at Alex and Sydney's weddings, too," I agree.

Victoria and Kevin parade onto the dance

floor, wrap their arms around each other, and start swaying back and forth to "All You Need Is Love," which doesn't sound quite the same with Vicky's peculiar harpsichord-heavy band playing it instead of the Beatles, but I guess it's the thought that counts.

After a few minutes, the band leader says into the microphone, "And now, the newlyweds would like to invite their wedding party to join them on the dance floor."

Leo holds out his hand to me, and I take it with an unsettling sense of disbelief, like this can't really be happening . . . is it actually possible to get through this without everything going horribly wrong?

We follow Sofia and Ben onto the dance floor and Leo puts one hand on my waist, holding me in the old-fashioned dance pose, which is strangely charming. And, of course, he turns out to be a great dancer. I'm pretty bad because I'm terrible at following—I'm never sure what's going on. But his moves are confident and his signals are really clear . . . and wow, if that isn't a metaphor for this relationship so far, I don't know what is.

"What are you smiling about?" he asks.

"You're a good dancer," I say, and he smiles down at me, pulling me closer. I can feel his body lightly pressed against mine and his hand moving gently in the small of my back, guiding me around the dance floor. My skin seems to be thrumming with heat, and I think I wouldn't mind if he whirled me through the nearest door, threw me down on the grass, and ripped this dreadful flower sack dress right off me. Of course he wouldn't, because he's a gentleman, but the thought makes my cheeks turn pink, and I scramble for a new item of conversation.

"I'm glad Victoria picked this song for her first dance," I say, "because I would never pick it myself in a million years."

"Me neither," he says. "It has sort of a poor rhythm for dancing to."

"Tell me about it," I agree. "And Alex and Sydney picked songs I wouldn't want, too, so at least there's one piece of the wedding that I'll be able to choose without worrying that it's been done before."

"You think about that a lot, don't you?" he says, and I guess my expression must have turned worried, because he quickly adds, "No, no, I think it's cute—and natural, believe me. When you're at a wedding, you can't help but think about what you'd do for your own. I'm pretty sure I was the only boy in sixth grade who had ever thought about what his first wedding dance should be."

I laugh. "What did you pick?"

"Oh, I'm definitely not telling you that."

"You have to!" I poke his shoulder. "Tell me, tell me!"

"Man . . . okay, but bear in mind I was twelve, and it was a different time then."

"Yeah, five years ago is simply ages," I tease.

"In pop music, it is!" he says. "Promise not to make fun."

"It depends on how awful it is."

"It's pretty awful."

I grin, and he sighs heavily. "All right," he

says. "I was thinking . . . 'I Want It That Way.'"

"The Backstreet Boys?" I cry, and then crack up. Luckily the song is over and people are milling around the dance floor, so no one is staring at us.

"Dude," he says, "I've matured a lot since then! I swear!"

Tears are actually running down my face, I'm laughing so hard. He rubs his hand through his dark hair sheepishly.

"All right, I can see I'm going to have to do something drastic to make you forget I just said that," he says. And then he grabs my hand and pulls me out through the long glass doors into the dark garden, and as I'm still catching my breath, he presses me against the wall, puts his hands on my waist, and kisses me.

"I love your laugh," he says, then kisses me again. "And your smile. And your eyes . . ."

"I—" I start to say, but then his mouth is on mine, and it's just as well, because the only thing I can think of to say is *I love you,* and that was by far the biggest mistake I made with David.

195

This is different, my mind says. *He's not David. Sofia was right. Stop worrying about the Wedding Curse . . . everything is going to be okay.*

I should have known better. I really, really should have known better.

Chapter Eleven

As my hands move across Leo's back and he starts to kiss my neck, suddenly there is an enormous crash from inside. I jump away from Leo like I've just touched an electric fence. We look at each other for a moment, startled, and then run back through the doors.

I don't know what I expected to see, but it's certainly not this: The clarinet player has his hands around the violist's throat, and they are staggering back and forth, knocking over the rest of the band's instruments, shouting, and throwing punches at each other.

"What are you *doing*?" Victoria shrieks. "Stop it, stop it right now!"

Leo grabs one of my hands. "Don't even think it," he says. "This isn't your fault, Jack."

"Are you kidding me?" I say. "Do you see this? Did you notice that timing?"

The fighting band members crash into the harpsichord, and the harpsichordist leaps to his feet and joins the fray. The bandleader is yelling and waving his arms, as are several members of my family, but it doesn't do any good.

To my immense surprise, Kevin dives in and tries to separate them, which makes me respect him a little bit more. Of course, he instantly gets punched in the nose for his efforts and comes staggering back out. Victoria runs over to take care of him, but one of her tall heels wobbles and then breaks, and with a wild yelp, she trips and goes flying into the cake table, which collapses underneath her. The entire six-layer white chocolate wedding cake, daffodils and sugar flowers and all, comes cascading down on top of her.

Also on the table were six tall flickering candles. As Victoria comes floundering out, with frosting and cake plastered through her hair, I spot a burst of flame and realize that my sister's wedding dress is *on fire*.

Okay. I've never claimed to be smart. Remember, I said that way at the beginning. Sofia is the smart one. I am just a bridesmaid. And so, I do exactly what a bridesmaid ought to do when her bride's dress is on fire, which is to say, the opposite of what any sane person would do.

Yes, I am the one closest to her. Who knows whether anyone else would have been this dumb if I hadn't moved first? But basically, I throw myself at Vicky, knocking us both to the ground, and roll on her dress to put the flames out. It's not a heroic thing to do, believe me. A hero would have taken a moment to think about what he or she was doing, and then it probably would have occurred to said hero to grab a tablecloth from any of the twenty nearby tables to throw on top of her instead of one's own body.

In fact, that's exactly what Leo does when *my*

dress, which is apparently made of gunpowder or something, bursts into flame a second later.

The last thing I hear is Vicky screaming, and the last thing I feel is Leo's strong arms wrapped around me and the tablecloth, lifting me up, before I pass out, and then . . . darkness.

I wake up in a cool, white, quiet space and for a minute I wonder if this is heaven, because I haven't been anywhere this peaceful—nor have I felt this rested—in a long time.

But then I turn my head and see Leo and Sofia sitting next to the bed, and I realize that my hands are wrapped in bandages, and they kind of hurt, and also the air smells like medicine and old people. That's enough clues for me to guess hospital.

"Jack!" Sofia cries, leaning forward in her chair. Leo wakes up instantly, and I like how tousled and funny his hair looks after sleeping in a chair.

"Is Vicky okay?" I ask.

"You big goof," Sofia says, but it looks like

she's trying not to cry. "She's totally fine. Do you know how many petticoats she was wearing? That dress could have been on fire for two hours and it wouldn't have gotten anywhere near her."

"Awesome," I say. "Glad I could help."

"Superman's got nothin' on you," Leo says with a smile.

"I'm going to call Mom and Dad," Sofia says, getting to her feet. "They had to go back to deal with—well, pretty much everything. But they said to call as soon as you woke up. Are you feeling all right?"

"A little woozy," I say, "but strangely blissful. Does that make sense?"

"I think that's the painkillers talking," Leo says.

Sofia leaves the room and Leo pulls his chair closer to the bed.

"Best date ever, huh?" I say. He smiles, gently takes one of my bandaged hands between his, and leans toward my face.

"Oh no," I say, putting my other hand quickly

in his way. "No way. Are you serious? Did you not see what happened? I completely ruined Victoria's wedding."

"No," he says, "the fact that the violist was sleeping with the clarinet player's wife ruined Victoria's wedding. That has nothing to do with you."

"I *am* the one that got set on fire," I point out. "That would seem to have something to do with me."

"You have noble instincts," he says. "That doesn't mean you're cursed."

"I cannot believe you don't believe in the Wedding Curse, after all that," I say. I'm trying to joke about it, but inside I'm feeling horribly, horribly guilty. Was one kiss on the terrace worth ruining my sister's wedding? I don't think so. I should have been stronger. She must be devastated, and it's all my fault, and there's nothing I can do about it. "Poor Victoria. Was she really mad?"

"My mom stayed with her to calm her down," Leo says, "while the rest of us came to the hospital with you."

"For a couple of little burns?" I say.

"Well, you were also unconscious." He points to a bandage on my head that I hadn't noticed before. "That had us all a little worried." Now I vaguely remember whanging my head really hard on a column as I fell.

"Bah," I say. "They should have stashed me in a corner and carried on with the reception. I'd've been fine."

He chuckles, and then Sofia comes back in, holding her cell phone. "Your mom wants to talk to you," she says to Leo. "I think she needs your help rescuing favors, organizing guests, stuff like that."

"All right," he says, standing up. "I'll come see you tomorrow." He leans down and quickly kisses my forehead, then steps out the door with Sofia's cell phone.

Sofia sits down in his chair. She still looks sort of wobbly and sad, so I reach over and pat her hand.

"It's okay, Sofia," I say. "See, I'm all right. I'm

203

just an idiot. Nothing serious."

She bursts into tears.

"I'm a terrible person," she sobs. "A terrible, awful person."

"Oh no," I say, pushing myself up and wincing in pain. "Sofia, *shh*, it's okay. You're not terrible, not at all. You're completely the opposite of terrible. What's wrong?"

"You're in the *hospital*," she says, hiccupping. "You got set on *fire*, and all I can think about is my own stupid relationship problems."

"Uh-oh," I say. "What happened?"

"No, we should focus on you," she says, shaking her head and breathing in deeply.

"Um, no," I say. "There's nothing to say about me. Blah, blah, set on fire, end of story. What happened with Ben?"

"I think we broke up," Sofia says, her eyes beginning to fill again.

As if I didn't feel awful enough already. "Oh no," I say softly.

"He wanted me to come to England with him in the fall," she says. "He made a joke about what our wedding would be like, and which song we'd play for our first dance, and I said something about him jumping ahead a little, and he said why not, because we love each other, and so I should come be with him when summer's over and postpone grad school for a year, but then I said I wasn't sure because we only just got back together and what if it all ends suddenly again, and *he* asked why I didn't believe in us and *I* said it just felt terrible when it ended last time and I'd thought he was committed *then* and then he got all upset about my lack of commitment *now* and whether I even really cared about him at all and I said of course I do but if I go to England that'll be me taking a huge commitment leap while he wouldn't be doing anything that crazy and then he left and then you got set on fire, and it was pretty much all downhill from there."

Neither of us says it, but I'm sure she's thinking about the Wedding Curse just as much as I am. I guess there's two ways it can manifest— obvious disaster, like seagulls and mumps and what happened with Patrick at Alexandria's wedding and the fire tonight—or emotional wreckage, like what David did to me . . . or what Sofia is going through now.

"I'm sorry, Sofia," I say.

"Me too," she says. "Let's talk about something else."

"Okay." I think for a moment. "Do you have any idea how the clarinet player found out about the affair in the middle of Victoria's wedding?"

Sofia tries to hide a smile. "I think he saw a note scribbled on the violist's sheet music."

"Like what?" I ask. "Don't forget to sleep with Bob's wife later?"

She laughs. "I think it was actually *from* the wife. Like 'Ooh, Fred, your viola is so hot.' "

"I want you to tighten *my* strings, lots of love, p.s., don't tell Bob?" I guess.

We talk about that for a while, joking about the Yoko Ono of the wedding band, but our hearts aren't in it, and I'm getting tired. I manage to stay awake until Mom and Dad arrive, but soon after that, I conk out. At least while I'm sleeping, I don't have to feel the weight of the Wedding Curse pressing down on me . . . and I don't have to think about how to tell Leo I can't see him again.

Chapter Twelve

When I open my eyes the next morning, there is someone hovering over me. At first I hope it's Leo, and then I think it's a nurse, and then my eyes focus and I realize that it's Paris. Who . . . is not exactly the number one person I'm hoping to see right now.

"You're awake!" she says brightly. "Good. I thought since you're not doing anything else, you could help me with something."

"Nice to see you, too, Paris," I say. "Everything's fine, thanks for asking."

She empties a giant bag of stationery and stickers onto the covers. "Invitations!" she says gaily. "Won't this be fun?"

So, yes, I spend the next two days, after they let me go home, sitting in my bed folding Paris's handmade invitations, affixing stickers to them, dropping pressed flowers into the envelopes, sealing them, and stamping them. Luckily my hands are too wrapped in bandages for me to write out all the addresses for her as well.

"What on earth is this?" Leo asks, coming into my room to find me covered in flat flowers and bits of bright yellow tissue paper.

"You'll never guess," I say, accidentally scattering half the flowers to the floor, which has nothing to do with the nervous way my heart jumps when I see him, of course. "Oops."

"Here." He gathers everything off the floor and sits down on the bed beside me, rearranging the piles. I scan my room surreptitiously, but Sofia seems to have done a good job of hiding everything embarrassing, since we both figured Leo would be showing up soon.

"Leo—"

"Uh-oh," he says. "That's a serious voice."

"Yeah," I say. "I'm sorry. You're so great, and I like you so much, and I know you think I'm being really stupid, but I can't do this. I can't date you right now."

"Jack, you're just being superstitious," he says.

"Maybe," I say. *Or maybe I don't want my heart broken like Sofia's just was.* "But it amounts to the same thing. I'm serious about this."

Leo sighs heavily. He sits next to me for a moment, turning one of the invitations over in his hands and staring down at it as if his mind is somewhere far away. Finally he looks at me again and says, "Can I still help you with the invitations?"

"Really?" I say. "Even though I just rejected you?"

"Ouch," he says, pressing one hand to his heart. "I'd rather think of it as a postponement than a rejection."

"If you want to, of course you can help," I say. "But you'll have to sit over there." I point to the chair. Having the side of his body pressed against mine is already making me have all sorts of inappropriate thoughts about things that really shouldn't happen in places where my dad can walk in at any moment.

Leo gathers some of the invitation materials and sits down in the chair. The task goes a lot faster with him there, and soon we have a neat stack of stuffed, sealed envelopes. It's baffling how nice he is to me, considering how much I don't deserve it. And when we're finished, he bows gallantly and leaves without even stroking my hair or trying to kiss me. Which is good . . . right? That's what I want him to do.

I lean back on the pillows and sigh. I really hope life gets less complicated after high school.

Mom and Dad throw a celebratory dinner for me when I get the bandages taken off my hands, which is sweet but really unnecessary, since it's my own idiocy that got them put on in the first place.

"Wow—all my favorite foods," I say, sitting

down at the table. "If you're not careful, I'll start throwing myself on open flames more often."

Victoria is off on her honeymoon with Kevin, flitting around England and Scotland. Mom has talked to her a few times, and it sounds like the honeymoon is going much better than the wedding did, but Vicky's still pretty upset about it.

"Carolina was so distraught," Mom says. "She waived her fee for Vicky's wedding and gave us a discount for Paris's, even though I told her it clearly wasn't her fault."

"It's not like anyone could have predicted that," Sofia says. She's putting on a brave face, but I can tell she's still really shaken up about Ben.

"Vicky did say she never trusted that clarinet player," I point out.

"True, but it was the violist who was shady," Sofia says. "The clarinet player just has anger management issues."

"The good news," Paris says brightly from

her seat, "is that now we can all focus on *my* wedding."

"That *is* good news," I agree, but she is the only one at the table who doesn't catch the sarcasm.

"Of course, the important place to start is with your outfits," Paris says. A warning bell goes off in my head. It's definitely a bad sign that she's calling them "outfits" instead of dresses.

"Maybe we should have one night of not talking about weddings," Sofia suggests. "Since we're celebrating Jack's recovery and everything."

"What*ever*," Paris says. "Jack doesn't mind. Right, Jack?"

"Um . . . okay," I say, sticking to my "path of least resistance" strategy.

"Great," Paris says contentedly. "So, my vision for this wedding is SUNFLOWERS. Got that? Everything yellow! And sunny! And bright! In fact, I've made up my mind," she says to me with earnest enthusiasm, as if I've been worrying about this for *weeks*. "I'm going to dye my hair bright yellow for the wedding, just like the sunflowers."

Dad visibly winces.

"So . . . yellow dresses?" Sofia says hopefully.

"Even better," Paris says. "I mean, we're on a beach, right? So I'm thinking—overalls! With sunflower flip-flops and sunflower hair clips and bright yellow leotards underneath. Oh my goodness, it's going to be SO ADORABLE."

Now it's my turn to wince. Bright yellow leotards?

"Paris, are you sure?" Mom asks. "That's a little . . . unusual, isn't it?"

"Exactly!" Paris trills. "It all came to me, like in a VISION, like with my glassblowing. I know exactly how the whole thing should look. It'll be *perfect*."

Not if I bring a date, it won't. I'm half-tempted to do it, just as vengeance for making us wear leotards and overalls. If anyone deserves to fall into a cake and be set on fire, it's probably Paris. But nobody really deserves that. And I'm not a vengeful person. I'm a bridesmaid. I smile at Paris as sweetly as I can.

"Whatever you want, Paris," I say. "It's your wedding."

"Yes, it is," she says with satisfaction.

Chapter Thirteen

True to her word, Sofia plans the whole bachelorette party for Paris. I offer to help, but I'm very glad she turns me down, because finding a weekend when all ten of Paris's MOST IMPORTANT FRIENDS can be there is hard enough, and that's just the beginning.

"Do you think she wants to go out drinking?" Sofia worries. We're walking Dublin through the woods behind our house, trying to catch a moment away from Paris to talk about the plans, which Paris has decided *must* be a surprise. "Because you and I aren't getting into any bars that she would approve of."

"I think as long as there's a stripper, she'll

be happy," I say.

Sofia pales. "A *stripper*?" she cries. "Are you serious? Do I have to hire a stripper?"

"Don't worry," I say. "I'm sure that won't come up when they're debating your Supreme Court nomination."

Sofia smacks my arm. "I'm thinking no on strippers," she says. "Agreed?"

"You don't have to convince *me*."

"Maybe we can go to that pottery-making place in town," Sofia says. "We can all make cute pots and then go out for dinner."

"Sure, that's artsy," I say. "Paris would like that. You know, as long as there's a stripper for dessert."

"Stop with the stripper talk!" Sofia squeals, covering her ears.

"I'm just kidding," I say. "I think it sounds like fun."

But we haven't counted on Paris's crazy artist friends. Someone named Yolanda (screen name Monet666, whatever *that* means) insists that "our Paris" needs more than that for her "one and only bachelorette party" and then she and someone called Ivy (screen name PlathHead, which is almost more worrisome) assure us that they'll "take care of the rest of the night."

"All right," Sofia e-mails her back. "But Jack and I are under 21, and no strippers, please."

They don't write back to this, so there's not much we can do but cross our fingers and hope.

Paris does seem to think the pottery-making is "*adorable*," although she looks around a few times like she's expecting naked men to come swarming in. In broad daylight. In the middle of Main Street in our tiny, quiet town.

Afterwards we go to a cute Italian place in the next town for dinner. Yolanda suggested this instead of the Thai place my family likes. It turns out she picked it because they have a drinks menu with funny, scandalously named drinks just for bachelorettes, plus a wholly-inappropriate-for-innocent-minds-like-mine scavenger hunt you can play in the dimly lit bar at the back if you want to pay an extra fee for it.

A grim-looking bouncer stamps my hand and Sofia's hand so everyone knows we're underage, but he doesn't have to worry. Neither of us has any interest in drinking, especially with this crowd, and we both know we'll be driving them all home.

Yolanda, who turns out to be a curvy, tattooed girl with heavy eyeliner and big teeth, lets out a loud shriek of laughter when she sees the drinks list. Ivy—a tiny purple-haired sprite—is equally excited by the scavenger hunt. They all immediately order a round of the "Naked Fireman," a bright red drink with apparently gallons of rum in it, and it's at this stage that it becomes pretty clear to me and Sofia what the rest of the night is going to be like.

Indeed, it only takes Paris about two drinks to triple her decibel level and start throwing herself at random guys in the bar, demanding their boxers and phone numbers and other things that I'm pretty sure are not on the scavenger hunt list. Yolanda, Ivy, and the others think this is absolutely hysterical. Sofia and I try to focus on our gnocchi and pretend like we're not actually with them.

"I can't believe I'm getting MARRIED!" Paris shouts.

"BOOOO!" shout some of the more delightful bar guys.

"It's okay!" she yells back. "You can hook up with one of my sisters instead! See? They're both single!" She points helpfully at the two of us.

"Um, yeah, but I'm not legal!" I offer loudly—the loudest I will get tonight.

"You are so throwing me to the wolves," Sofia says, giving me a dirty look as one of the guys switches his leer from me to her.

"Don't you think they ought to know?" I say innocently. "I'm just performing a public service."

Eventually we make it out of the bar without being manhandled by barbarians, and we pile the screaming drunk girls into the two minivans we've borrowed for the night. Yolanda gives us muddled directions, and I nervously follow

Sofia's van as we make our way through dark streets to an apartment building, where, it turns out, Yolanda lives.

Her apartment is mysteriously covered in shredded newspaper and sound equipment. Yolanda stumbles around clearing space for us all to pile onto the two couches. I take one look at the stains on the upholstery and drag out a bar stool to perch on instead.

"Yolanda is an ARTIST," Paris announces. "Just like ME!"

"I work with paper collage and music," Yolanda says, nodding deeply.

"That is SO SEXY," Paris declares woozily.

"You know what else is sexy?" Yolanda says. "STRIPPERS!" She flings open the door and reveals two burly men in flimsy-looking police-man costumes. They sashay through the door and do a spin, pulling their shirts aside to give us a peek at their smooth chests.

"WOOOOOOOOOOOOOOOOOOOOO!" Paris screeches.

I bolt for the stairs. I'm sorry, I know this is

typical bachelorette party stuff, and I know I'm fully seventeen and shouldn't have a problem with naked men and should probably think this is hilarious and fun, but no, seriously, I really, really don't want strange guys shaking their booties anywhere near me, especially when those strange guys have mustaches and remind me of my uncle Stan, who is a real cop with an outfit that doesn't tear off (at least, I hope not, although thanks very much for that brain-scarring image, YOLANDA).

I make it all the way to the street before Sofia catches up with me.

"Ack!" she yelps, wriggling in disgust. "It's like she didn't even *read* my e-mail!"

"To be fair, she's probably right that this is what Paris would want," I point out. "But I would rather wear a bright yellow leotard every day for the rest of my life than go back up there right now."

"I know, I know," Sofia frets, chewing on a fingernail. "But we can't leave. We're the desig-nated drivers. I shudder to think how they'd get home otherwise. I mean, they might throw themselves at guys on the street for a ride, and that's the best case scenario."

"Can we just sit out in the cars until they're done?" I offer hopefully.

"It could be *hours*," Sofia points out.

"I don't mind," I say stoutly, climbing into the driver's seat of my minivan. "You can go back upstairs if you want. I'll just nap right here."

"I'm not leaving you alone," Sofia says, but she looks torn.

"We both know someone sober should probably be keeping an eye on Paris up there," I say, shutting the door and rolling down the window to talk to her. "You go ahead. Don't worry about me."

"Could we call someone?" she suggests. "To come sit with you?"

Of course, the same person occurs to us both simultaneously. "No," I say, pointing sternly at her. "I told him we can't date. I can't then call him and ask him to come sit in a parked car on a dark street with me for, like, five hours. That's weird and confusing and it sends a mixed message and . . . bad, Sofia, bad!"

"Not if we explain what's happening," Sofia says. She already has her cell phone out. "We'll tell Carolina to pay him for it, and add it to Paris's fee. It's the least Paris can do."

"So now we're paying him to come hang out with me?" I rest my head on my elbows in the window frame as she dials. "That's really pretty pathetic."

"But it makes it a professional interaction," Sofia points out, lifting the phone to her ear. "So I'm sure he'll behave himself. Hello? Carolina? We have a tiny problem, and we were wondering if you could help, since you're so lovely."

She paces beside the car as she explains the situation, and finally she hangs up with a smile. "All taken care of," she says. "He'll be here in five minutes."

Don't be excited. Stop being excited. Heart, shut the heck up.

"All right," I say, trying to sound nonchalant.

"You can go back upstairs."

"Are you sure?" she asks.

"Absolutely," I say. "Have fun with the strippers. And try not to think of Uncle Stan."

"Oh, thanks very much!" Sofia cries, pressing her fists into her eyes. "Jack! Gross!" She reluctantly heads back to the apartment. I'm still giggling a few minutes later when Leo's hybrid car pulls up in front of mine and parks. He swings out of the driver's seat and saunters to my window.

"Hey there," he says in a saucy voice. "How much for an hour?"

"At least two thousand bucks," I joke.

He whistles. "Okay, what if I just want you to paint my nails and let me wear your heels?"

"Oh, in that case it's three thousand," I say, thinking with amusement that I'm glad I have proof that he's not gay.

"Those must be some heels," he says. "What about just talking?"

"That's free," I say, patting the passenger seat beside me. He walks around and climbs in.

"So you're having a crazy night, huh?" he says. There are a few hideously white streetlights lighting up the road, so we're not totally in the dark, but it's still hard not to think about the kiss at the wedding. Leo stays politely in his corner, though, not even reaching over to smooth back my hair like he sometimes does.

"Yeah," I say. "I wasn't invited to this part of Alex's and Sydney's bachelorette parties, what with being only fourteen and fifteen and all. I'm pretty sure neither of them had strippers, either."

"Well, if any of your sisters were going to, I'd guess Paris . . ." he says.

"I know. I'm sure she's having a great time. But I'm pretty glad I'm down here." *With you*, I almost add.

"Me too," he says. "I mean, we wouldn't want your purity sullied or anything. That might drop your price under two thousand."

"Shut up," I say, punching his shoulder. "It's gross, and you know it."

"They're just working guys trying to make a

living," he says with a grin.

"Have you ever been to a strip club?" I ask.

"Nope. One of the grooms this summer invited me along to his bachelor party, but I said no."

"Wow. You're so civilized," I say, tipping my seat back. "David would have gone in a heartbeat. I think he managed to get into a strip club when he was fourteen." The moon roof on the minivan is open so we can see the stars—at least, the few that are bright enough to battle the streetlights. Leo leans back in his seat, too, and we both look up at the sky.

"Jack," he says after a minute, "is your Wedding Curse thing really about seagulls crashing your sister's wedding?"

"And hotels burning down," I point out. "And mumps and lightning. And flower allergies."

"But is that really it?" he says. "Or was it the guys you took to those weddings? I mean—no offense, but they don't sound like the best two first boyfriends."

I haven't even told him that much about

Patrick and David. I mean, Patrick was one thing . . . he was just a gawky teenage boy with acne who got overwhelmed by the whole wedding thing and my big insane family. But I thought David was real. I told him I loved him. I thought he loved me. At Sydney's wedding, when he got really drunk and tried to convince me to sneak off and lose my virginity to him in a broom closet, I nearly did it. I thought it would be the only way to keep him . . . but luckily that thought stopped me from doing it. That, and him vomiting in the museum fountain. Which, incidentally, didn't stop him from going back in and trying to hook up with my cousin Wendy, who was twenty-two at the time.

As I've mentioned before, David broke up with me the next day—at the post-wedding brunch, no less. Maybe he wouldn't have done that if I'd slept with him, but I still think it was probably the best decision I ever made. Besides, can you imagine? Sleeping with my date at a wedding? The Wedding Curse would probably have made the museum collapse into a sinkhole.

The whole state might have ended up underwater.

"Jack?" Leo says, and I realize I haven't said anything in a long time.

"Yeah, Patrick and David were pretty lame," I say.

"Maybe if you took a decent date to a wedding, the Wedding Curse would be lifted," Leo suggests.

"You mean like you?" I say, turning my head to smile at him. "Perhaps I should remind you that I *did* take you to Vicky's wedding, and look how that turned out."

"But that was under duress," he says mischievously. "Maybe the Wedding Curse wants you to make the wise choice yourself."

"Oh, you're the *wise* choice," I say. "I think the Wedding Curse might need to be a little clearer about what it wants, then. Like by not setting me on fire. That'd be a great start."

"My mom told me about a bride who set her stripper on fire at a bachelorette party like this," Leo says, nodding at Yolanda's apartment building.

We can see her window from here, and although the shades are closed, there are alarming silhouettes gyrating around behind them.

"She set her stripper on fire?" I echo. "Are you kidding? And it wasn't Paris? That sounds exactly like her. Maybe I should go back up there."

"I'm sure Sofia has hidden the matches and lighters," Leo says.

"And *I'm* sure Paris has some sort of flame-shooting glassblowing implement hidden in her purse," I say. "But somehow I can't bring myself to rush up there and rescue a couple of naked mustachioed men. Maybe I'm not a superhero after all."

"It's the thought that counts," Leo says comfortingly. "And if anything does happen, we'll see the flames from here. And then we can call someone else to rescue them."

"Knowing Yolanda, there are probably some 'firemen' lined up for later anyway," I joke. Leo has steered us back into safe conversational waters, and I'm glad he didn't press for more

information about David. I haven't told anyone but Sofia the whole story, and I don't
think I ever will. That was probably the point
when I decided that my family might be
insane, but they still deserve my loyalty more
than any guy.

Leo tells me more wild stories of his mom's
clients' bachelorette parties, and I'm actually
surprised when Paris and her friends come
spilling out of the apartment and I realize three
hours have gone by.

"Wow," I say, looking at my watch. "It's really
late. I'm so sorry."

"No worries," he says. "This was more fun
than what my mom would have had me
doing—probably filing receipts or printing out
directions for next weekend's wedding."

"I keep forgetting you have other clients
besides us," I say, watching Paris drunkenly
careen toward the car.

"Sadly, we do," he says gallantly. "Do you
want me to follow you guys home? Or take
someone in my car?"

"Thanks, but it's all right," I say. "We've got it from here."

"Okay," he says, hesitating with his hand on the door. "Good night, Jack."

"Good night, Leo."

And then he's gone—once again, as politely as possible, without a hint of romantic attraction toward me. Maybe he's over me. Or maybe he's just doing what I asked. It's my own fault I have no idea, of course, and I am fully aware of that.

"OH MY GOD," Paris shrieks as she clambers into the passenger seat. "You missed the BEST SHOW, Jack. It was SO HOT. I LOVE STRIPPERS! WOOOOO!" She screams this last bit out the car window, and several people on the street turn to stare at us.

Luckily, Paris conks out before we drop everyone else off and get home. So at least there's no screaming "I LOVE STRIPPERS!" on our front lawn, which Mom and Dad would probably have frowned upon. Of course, it also means that Sofia and I have to heft her out of the car and carry her all the way up to her room.

We roll her into bed, take off her shoes, and scarper out into the hallway, where we collapse on the floor for a moment.

"Jack," Sofia whispers, "if I ever get married, promise me one thing."

"No strippers?"

"No strippers."

"Ice cream instead?"

"Sounds like a plan," she agrees. We head off to the kitchen, where two pints of Ben & Jerry's are waiting to make up for the rest of the night.

Chapter Fourteen

The strangest, craziest, best, and worst weekend of my life begins on a Thursday night in August, a week and two days before Paris's wedding. It's after eleven o'clock, and I'm lying in bed in the dark, watching *Wedding Crashers*, perhaps hoping that other people's hilarious wedding misadventures will make ours seem funnier, when my cell phone rings.

"Hello?"

"Hey, Jack." Leo's voice makes me smile. I pause the DVD and burrow farther under the covers.

"Hey yourself."

"Whatcha doin'?"

"Watching *Wedding Crashers*. In bed."

"Oooh," he says. "That sounds sexy."

I laugh. "Yeah, my pajamas are reeeeal sexy."

"I've seen them," he reminds me. "On you they are."

"Leo," I say warningly.

"In a friendly way," he says quickly. "Friendly-sexy. In a harmless, nonthreatening way. Sexy like a teddy bear. Or a cupcake. Or a moose."

"Okay, stop," I say, giggling.

Suddenly the door to my room opens. I'm not sure why, since I'm not doing anything wrong, but I fling the phone under the covers and put on an innocent face.

"Jack?" Sofia's voice whispers. She creeps in and shuts the door behind her. The glow from the paused DVD lights up her face as she tiptoes over to my bed. "Are you awake?"

"Yeah, totally," I say, flicking on the light beside my bed. I can see right away that something is happening. Her face is glowing and I've never seen such a huge smile. She sits down on the bed beside me and starts talking so fast, I don't have a chance to tell her I'm on the phone.

"We're doing it, Jack," she says, seizing my arm. "We're really doing it. And I want you to come with us, so get dressed, quick."

"Wait, what?" I say. "Come with you where? Doing what?"

Sofia leaps up and grabs my backpack from the floor. As she talks, she dumps out the contents and starts stuffing clothes into it.

"To Las Vegas!" she announces. "I'm eloping!" She turns to see my reaction, grinning widely.

I literally nearly fall out of the bed. "Are you serious? With who?"

"Ben, of course!" she says with a laugh. There's no "of course" about it to me. Last I heard they were over. Kaput. *Finito*. Right?

"But . . . in Las Vegas? Right *now*?"

"That's the whole idea of eloping," Sofia says. "And like we've always said, it's the one thing our sisters have never done."

"Except now you're doing it," I point out, smiling, "which leaves nothing for me to do."

She laughs. "Sorry," she says. "But it just feels right, you know?"

I don't really. I can't imagine just handing my heart over like that, after everything they've been through, and while she's still so young. But she's Sofia, and she's my brilliant, gifted, genius sister, so I'll believe in anything she wants to do. Plus—Vegas!

"I'm so there," I say, jumping out of bed and taking the backpack from her. "But what about Mom and Dad?"

"I'll call them when we get there," she says. "Isn't this exciting? We're just running off in the middle of the night! My heart is pounding so hard right now, is yours?"

Her enthusiasm is kind of infectious. "I should pack something nice to wear," I say. "For the ceremony."

"I always said you'd get to pick your own dress for my wedding, didn't I?" Sofia says. "See, I'm keeping my promise. No dreadful bridesmaid dresses here."

"I knew you would," I say, smiling. "But wait, tell me what happened. How did you go from broken up to engaged, like, overnight?"

"I went out to walk Dublin," she says, her eyes dreamy, "and he was waiting outside, and he said that he's been thinking about it, and I'm right—if I'd be willing to go to England for him, he should do something to prove his commitment too. And then he got down on one knee and asked me to marry him!"

"Wow," I say, dropping a pair of nice shoes into my backpack. "It just seems so . . . sudden."

"You don't think it's too fast, do you?" Sofia says anxiously. "I'm not being stupid, am I? I mean, it's *Ben*. He's the Love of My *Life*. I'm not being Paris, right? This is totally different?"

"It is different," I say, "because it's you, and you don't do wild and crazy things like Paris. By definition, if you're doing it, it's not a stupid thing to do."

"Oh, thank you!" Sofia says, throwing her arms around my neck before I can get to the "but" part of my statement. Because . . . this does still seem kind of insane. "I knew you'd understand," she rattles on. "This is going to be so much fun."

"Paris is going to kill us for disappearing right before her wedding," I say.

"We'll be back by Sunday, which is still plenty of time," Sofia says. "And we suffered through her insane bachelorette party, so she can't be too mad."

"True."

"All right, I'm going to finish grabbing my stuff," Sofia says. "Be careful not to wake Mom and Dad or Paris, okay? And meet me outside as soon as you're ready—Ben's waiting to drive us all to the airport."

"Wow, you really do mean right now," I say faintly.

"That is the whole point," she says again, beaming. "You're the best sister ever, Jack." And then she flies out the door, leaving me feeling a bit like I've been tossed around in a blender.

I look around for my cell phone, at which

point I suddenly remember that I never hung up on Leo, and he probably heard that entire conversation.

"Leo?" I stage-whisper into the phone, huddling behind the bed in case Sofia comes charging back in.

"Wow," he says. "That's . . . wow."

"So you heard all that?" I say.

"Your family really is crazy," he says.

"I can't believe this is happening," I say back. "Promise not to tell anyone."

"Are you kidding?" he says. "I've been packing this whole time. I'll meet you at the airport."

My jaw drops in disbelief.

"Hello?" he says. "Jack?"

"What . . . what do you mean? At the airport?"

"I'm coming with you guys," he says, as if that's obvious. "Don't worry, I'll pay for my own ticket. I've earned enough working for Mom this summer."

"I hardly think that's the issue," I say. "The issue is that you're not invited. I mean, what

240

would Sofia say if you turned up?"

"I think she'll be happy," Leo says. "She obviously hasn't thought this through."

"Well . . . that's true in a lot of ways."

"For instance, where are you supposed to stay while Sofia and Ben enjoy their newly wedded bliss? In a hotel room in Las Vegas by yourself?"

"Um . . ." I hadn't thought of that. "I'm not sure a hotel room with *you* will make my parents feel any better about all this."

"You think they'll care? Considering that your other sister is, like, eloping? Listen, Jack, if this is what you're really worried about, I promise not to try anything. I'll be a perfect gentleman, I swear. I just think you'll need someone there to look out for you. Newlyweds are cute and all, but they have a tendency to forget there's anyone else around."

I press my hands to my temples. He has a point. I can't imagine what it's going to be like in Vegas with just those two. I'll be worse than a third wheel, no matter how great Sofia is about it.

And it would be pretty amazing to have Leo there . . . so I wouldn't be alone . . . just as long as I can resist the temptation to—

"All right," I say. "Okay."

"Really?" he says with delight.

"Yes. I want you to come. If . . . you won't get in trouble with your mom?"

"She'll understand," he says. "The power of love, sweeping them off their feet, et cetera, et cetera."

"I better go," I say.

"See you soon," he says, and I swear I can hear him smiling.

I really do try to tell Sofia about Leo in the car, but she is chattering on about Las Vegas and which chapel they should use, and it's impossible to get a word in edgewise. So it's a bit of a surprise to her when we come up from the airport parking lot and find Leo lounging gallantly by the check-in desk. His sunglasses are pushed up on his head and he looks a little sleepy, but when he spots me he smiles and stands up straight.

"Um. What?" Sofia says to me, raising her eyebrows and pointing at him as we walk through the doors.

"I'm sorry," I say. "He was on the phone when you came in, so he heard, and he wanted to come . . ."

"The more, the merrier," Ben says brightly, squeezing her arm. "Since my brother is stuck in England, maybe Leo can be my best man." He has a really cute way of saying "Leo" in his adorable accent that almost makes me forgive him for how sad Sofia has been this past month.

"Okay," Sofia says with a shrug, and miraculously, that is all there is to it, because, as I have said before, this particular sister is wonderful. She can pretty much handle anything that gets thrown at her.

"I hear congratulations are in order," Leo says to Sofia as we join him. "I hope you don't mind me crashing the party." He casually brushes a strand of hair out of my eyes, then drops his hand quickly, as if he wants to keep touching me but knows he shouldn't.

243

"No problem; it'll be fun," she says cheerfully. "Were you able to get on the flight?"

"I didn't book it yet because I wanted to make sure it was the same one you have," Leo says, following her up to the counter. They lean over and start talking to the woman behind the desk, leaving me and Sofia's fiancé (ACK!) with the bags.

Ben winks at me. "That bloke's quite besotted with you, isn't he?" he says.

"Leo's just a friend," I say.

"Sure," he says. "But I tell you, that look is exactly how I feel about Sofia."

Luckily, Leo and Sofia come back to us before I have to protest too much. We hustle through the airport because the flight is already boarding, so before I know it, I'm squeezed into a window seat with Leo right beside me and Sofia and Ben behind us, and the airplane is taxiing down the runway.

"See?" Leo whispers. "You'd have had to sit by yourself if I weren't here. Or with somebody HUUUUGE."

"This from the guy who is blatantly hogging the armrest," I say, nudging his arm aside. "What did you bring to read?"

"To read?" he says. "Um . . . well, there's always the SkyMall catalog." He pulls it out of the seat pocket in front of him.

"Oh, please. You're traveling with an experienced flyer here," I say. "I brought a wide selection of reading options—everything from *Animal Farm* to *Cosmopolitan*—plus every episode of *The Office* and *Heroes* on my video iPod, plus playing cards and Uno. Trust me, we're well prepared for this trip."

He laughs. "How did you have time for that?"

"I'm always ready to drop everything and fly somewhere at a moment's notice," I say. "Our parents kind of trained us that way."

I can hear Sofia and Ben giggling and whispering to each other. Suddenly the awful realization hits me that if they're getting married, that means she'll be going off to England with him in the fall. England is a lot more than two hours away. Who knows when I'll get to see her again?

As if he can hear my thoughts, Leo takes my hand and squeezes it reassuringly. Then he squeezes it a little harder, and a little harder.

"Okay, ow," I say, looking at him. He's got his eyes closed and he looks sort of pale. "Are you all right?"

"I'll be fine once we're in the air," he says, and I realize we're taking off.

"Are you afraid of flying?" I tease.

"Not so much flying," he says, "just taking off and landing. Oh, and crashing. Mostly crashing. All the parts where the plane is really close to the ground but not actually on it."

"Well, I'll take care of you," I say, patting our linked hands.

I have to admit, the flight is a lot more fun with him there, and it probably would have been really weird with just Sofia and Ben. I mean, I love her, but I'm freaked out enough . . . at least Leo helps keep my mind off what we're going there to do.

Las Vegas is very bright and very colorful and there are a million flashing lights everywhere, even though it's a few hours from dawn when we arrive and it's pouring rain. We take a taxi from the airport, with the lights of the casinos flashing across our faces and reflecting in the raindrops on the windows. Sofia leans against Ben and he puts his arm around her, drawing her closer. In the front seat, Leo turns around to smile at me.

Despite how tired I am, it's still kind of a thrill to walk into our hotel and see how decked out and ridiculous the place is. I mean, there are *lions* in the lobby. Real live *lions*. *Seriously.*

Sofia suddenly looks worried. "I only reserved two rooms," she says softly to me. "I was going to give you one of them, but I guess maybe I could stay with you, and Ben and Leo could take the other room . . ."

"No, no, no," I say. "Don't be silly. This is your wedding weekend. You and Ben should have your own room. I don't mind staying with Leo—he promised to behave himself."

"Only if you want him to," Sofia says mischievously.

"I *do* want him to. Behave himself, I mean. I'm sure he will."

"Okay. If you're sure you're all right with this."

"*So* totally all right," I say. She goes to check in, and I glance over at Leo, who is standing by the lions looking a little bit awestruck. I am sure Leo will behave himself . . . but what about me? Am I so sure that *I* will? He does look really hot, especially since he's wet from the rain. His dark curls are slicked back and glistening, and his T-shirt is plastered to his chest, outlining the firm muscles underneath.

Um. Stop thinking about this RIGHT NOW.

I make myself look at the lions instead. Ooooh, lions.

In the elevator I start to feel sort of awkward, which Sofia might sense, because she turns to me when it stops on their floor.

"Are you sure you're okay?" she says.

"Absolutely. What's the plan for tomorrow?

248

Or, you know, actually today." I'm trying to look supportive and confident instead of concerned and slightly alarmed like I really feel.

"We should sleep in," she says, "which I'm sure you'll appreciate."

"This is already the best wedding ever," I say fervently.

She laughs. "Ben and I will go out and get our marriage license in the morning," she says. "Then we'll pick a chapel and call you when we get back. Is that okay?"

"You bet," I say, maybe a little too cheerfully, because once the doors close behind them, Leo takes my shoulders, shakes me lightly, and says, "Don't be nervous. I told you I'd be good."

"I know," I say. "I trust you." It's *me* I don't trust, but I don't tell him that.

He follows me quietly down the hall and waits while I swipe us into the room. There are two queen-sized beds and a positively gigantic TV taking up the opposite wall.

"You'd think they wouldn't want you to stay in your room and watch TV," I say, pointing at it.

"Maybe you can gamble through the TV somehow," he says, picking up the remote.

"Maybe tomorrow," I say, collapsing on the bed. "Is it really getting light outside already?"

Leo closes the curtains, and we listen to the patter of raindrops against the glass for a moment. Then he goes into the bathroom to brush his teeth, and when he's done I go in, and by the time I come back out, he's already curled up in one of the beds, apparently fast asleep.

I watch him for a moment, thinking about the feel of his hands and how soft his hair is. *Go to sleep, Jack,* my mind says. *He's helping you avoid temptation. And you're certainly tired enough. Stop thinking about kissing him and go to sleep.*

I climb into the other bed, surround myself with pillows, and fall asleep surprisingly quickly, considering there's a hot guy only a few feet away from me. In my dreams, it's me and Leo who are eloping, and as I stand across from him with an Elvis impersonator droning

at us, I suddenly realize I'm not wearing anything, and neither is he (although, luckily, the
Elvis impersonator is fully clothed), and let's
just leave the rest of the dream to your imagination.

Chapter Fifteen

"Jack?" A hand is stroking my shoulder softly. "Jack, wake up." The hand moves to my hair, smoothing it back from my face, and part of me is really tempted to pretend to keep sleeping, just to see what he'll do next. But my self-control prevails, and I open my eyes and roll over, blinking.

Leo is sitting on the edge of my bed, his hair rumpled with sleep. And he is *shirtless*. I tell you, I think he's torturing me.

"It's, like, two o'clock in the afternoon," he says, looking amused.

"Have you been awake for long?"

"Long enough to read *Animal Farm*," he says,

waving it at me.

"I guess it's lucky I didn't bring *War and Peace*," I say, leaning up on my elbows, "or you might have let me sleep until next year."

"You looked so peaceful," he says. "And your sister still hasn't called."

"Really?" That wakes me up a bit more. "That's weird."

"I'm sure she slept late, too," he says. "But maybe you should call her."

Nobody answers her room phone, and her cell phone goes straight to voice mail. I leave her a worried message and hang up.

"Hey, Vegas is crazy," Leo says. "I'm sure she's all right. She'll call soon."

"Yeah, she will," I agree. It is still pouring outside; I can hear thunder crashing and the splatter of the raindrops on the window.

"Apparently this is some freak weather," Leo says. "It never rains this much in Las Vegas. But," he says quickly, perhaps sensing what I'm about to say, "it's good luck to have rain on your wedding day, so this is definitely not a curse thing."

"Sure," I say, giving him a wry look.

"I mean, it can't be, right?" he says, spreading his hands. "We're being so well-behaved."

I'm not sure the thoughts I'm having about your shirtlessness are exactly "well-behaved," but okay. "Well, I'm going to shower," I say, "in case she calls and wants us to be ready to go right away."

After I emerge, my wet hair wrapped in towels, Leo takes his turn showering while I get dressed. I decide to wear the dress I've picked out for Sofia's ceremony, because my guess is that we'll have to race out the door as soon as she calls. It's my favorite dress, and I've only worn it once—to junior prom, which I attended with a big group of my single friends.

It's made of dark red silk that picks up on the highlights in my hair, which normally looks brown, but kind of has an auburn thing going when I wear this dress. It has a loose scoop neck and is fitted through the waist, then flares out to a knee-length skirt. There are tiny black jet beads sewn along the hem in a vine pattern. I'm kind of psyched to be able to wear it again. I just hope Sofia calls soon . . . this is not a dress for sitting around a hotel room in.

Leo comes out of the bathroom in just his jeans, toweling off his hair. He looks up and sees me, and his eyes soften in this really dreamy way. "Wow," he says. "You're not going to make it easy for a guy to behave himself, are you?"

Um, yeah, and the shirtless *thing is helping?* "See what a difference it makes when I get to dress myself?" I joke, twirling around. "Turns out I don't look terrible in everything . . . just in anything my sisters pick out."

"Are you trying to tell me you're not totally looking forward to the overalls at Paris's wedding?" Leo teases.

"Don't remind me." I roll my eyes. "I've been looking forward to choosing my own dress for Sofia's wedding . . . I just didn't think it would happen this soon."

"Don't worry," he says, hanging the towel up behind the door. "Sofia's a smart girl. She can take care of herself."

"I hope so," I say, rubbing my arms. "Are you starving? I'm starving. But we shouldn't leave, in case Sofia shows up looking for us. . . ."

"*Voilà!*" he says triumphantly, producing a room service menu from the desk.

"Ooooh," I say. "But . . . um, expensive, don't you think?"

"Will you let me buy you lunch?" he says. "I mean, most of the money I've made this summer was thanks to your family, honestly."

"When you put it that way—" I say, laughing. I choose a Cobb salad and he orders a grilled chicken sandwich. They arrive on a hilariously fancy rolling table with fancy silverware, a fancy white tablecloth, and posh silver lids we can whisk off as if we're in *Beauty and the Beast*. We roll it over to the end of Leo's bed and watch TV while we eat, perched on the edge of the mattress.

It does not escape my attention that we are sitting on a bed, very close to each other. But he keeps his promise and doesn't even touch me accidentally.

256

We are watching a show about meerkats on Animal Planet and joking about how silly they look when my cell phone finally rings. It's Sofia—thank goodness. It doesn't occur to me until just that moment that I have no idea what I would say if Mom or Dad, or most terrifying of all, Paris, called.

"Sofia!" I cry into the phone. "Where are you?"

"We're at a diner down the street from the hotel," Sofia says. She sounds more subdued than she did last night. "But I think we found the perfect chapel."

"Tell me there are Elvis impersonators," I say. She laughs.

"Sadly, no," she says. "But it's really cute! You'll like it."

"So should we meet you there soon?" I ask.

"Um . . ." she says hesitantly. "Well, we're still figuring that out. I'm thinking maybe later tonight. Would that be okay? Can you hang out until then? Maybe we can get married and then all have dinner together."

"Sure," I say. "Whatever you want to do. Do you want to do something together for the afternoon?"

"Well . . . Ben and I are kind of talking," Sofia says.

"Is everything okay?"

"Yeah, totally, of course," she says, but it's not very convincing. "We're just figuring out some stuff."

"Is there anything I can do?"

"Do you mind just hanging out for a while? And we'll call you later with the details of where to go and all that . . . would that be okay?"

"Absolutely," I say. She's repeating herself, so I can tell she's distracted. "Do whatever you have to do. Don't worry about me. But I'm here if you need me for any reason."

"Thanks, Jack," she says, sounding relieved. "Sorry to be all weird. I'm glad you have Leo there to entertain you."

"Yeah, we're doing fine," I say, glancing at him. He is finally wearing a shirt, by the way, and he's lying on the bed watching me alertly.

When he sees me look over at him, he winks. "Hey, Sofia, did you call Mom and Dad?"

"I did," she says. "But, um, I maybe didn't tell them everything."

"What did you say?"

"I told them you and I just needed to get away for a weekend, and we'd be back on Sunday."

"Did you even tell them where we are?"

"Um . . . no."

"Wild," I say. "They didn't care?"

"They seemed to have enough going on," she says. "I could hear Paris yelling in the background. Dad said maybe we should stay through next weekend, too, and she really didn't appreciate that."

"I guess they trust you," I say. She doesn't respond for a minute, so I add, "Which they should, Sofia. You're amazing."

"Do you think they'll be mad about this?" she says softly.

"I think they'll understand," I say. "Maybe not right away, but eventually."

"Hmm," she says. "All right. Call you soon."

"Have fun!" I say, and then we hang up. I put the phone back on the bedside table and smooth down my skirt.

"All dressed up and nowhere to go," I say ruefully.

"So let's go for a walk," Leo says, sitting up. "I've never been here. I've heard some of the hotels are off the charts."

"I've heard that, too," I say. "But we have to be careful—the gambling age is twenty-one, so they'll throw us out of any casinos."

"In that dress," he says, "I bet you could pass for twenty-one."

I smile and stand up. "Let's not risk it."

A couple of hours later, we get back to the room, laughing, hyper, and soaking wet. Well, Leo is soaking wet. He has gallantly thrown his raincoat over me to protect my dress and my hair, since I was dumb enough not to bring any sort of rainproof clothing along, despite my travel-happy upbringing.

We stumble through the door just as lightning illuminates the room, and I catch a glimpse of his dripping hair and his white teeth as he grins widely. He closes the door behind us and we stand for a moment in the dark, catching our breath.

"So, wow," I say. "Fountains, flamingos, and tigers, oh my."

"I liked the shark reef," he says. "That was crazy."

"And the volcano!" I say. My phone rings and I scramble to get it out of my purse.

"Hello?"

"Hey, Jack." It's Sofia again. "So . . . would you totally kill me if I said we're still talking?"

"Of course not," I say. "But haven't you run out of stuff to say yet?"

She chuckles. "Not quite. We're thinking maybe we'll get married tomorrow instead. Is that okay?"

I look down at my dress. "Sure. Just tell us what you want us to do."

"I'll call you in the morning," she says with a sigh. "Sorry again."

"Dude, whatever," I say. "We're having so much fun. Don't worry about us."

"You're the best," she says. "Have a good night."

I close the phone and look up at Leo. Neither of us has turned on the light yet, but I can see the outline of his face in the glow from the flashing signs outside.

"I should hang up my coat," I say.

"You mean *my* coat," he teases. He reaches out to help tug it off my shoulders, and his hands brush my bare arms. But he quickly pulls back, reaching for a coat hanger and putting the rain jacket into the closet beside us.

I move away a little, kicking off my shoes and wringing out my hair. He starts to step forward and I stop him with one hand on his chest.

"Stay there. Take off your shoes," I say. He obeys while I go into the bathroom and return with one of the big fluffy hotel towels. When I come back, I discover that he's also taken off his socks and his shirt, so he's once again just standing there in blue jeans, although this time he's much more wet.

"Thanks," he says with a smile, reaching for the towel. I bat his hands aside and wrap the towel around his chest, rubbing him dry. He stands very still as I move up to his face and his hair. I bring the towel back down to his waist and stop, my heart thundering in my chest, my breathing suddenly faster. Only a fold of terry cloth separates my hands from his bare skin. He's breathing more quickly, too, and through the towel I can feel that he's trembling a little.

"I'm sorry," he says, catching my hands as if to push me away. "I didn't mean to—I'm really trying—"

I drop the towel, run my hands up his chest, and kiss him. He kisses me back like he's drowning and I'm the air, but then he breaks away and steps back again. "No, I promised," he says. "I said I wouldn't—I really meant it."

"Don't you want to?" I say, touching his chest.

He lets out a breath. "You have no idea," he says. "But I don't want you to feel like I tricked you or anything when I said I'd be good. I only want to do what you want to do."

"I want to do this," I say, and kiss him again, harder this time. He runs his hands up my back to the triangle of bare skin below my neck and presses me into his lips.

"Jack, are you sure?" he says when we come up for air.

I've never felt so sure. I know how different this is, because I came this close with David and then stopped. I knew that was wrong . . . and I know this is right. Leo runs his hands along the curves of my waist and kisses the side of my neck as I lead him over to the bed.

"Jack," he whispers as we lie down, "I think I've loved you since the moment I—"

"Shhh," I say, and then . . . there's no more talking.

Chapter Sixteen

I wake up curled in Leo's arms, all the covers tossed aside. It's pitch dark outside, but it's stopped raining. His breathing in his sleep is calm, slow, and relaxing, and I match mine to it, realizing that I don't feel tense, probably for the first time in months. I rest my head on his shoulder and think about Sofia and Ben.

Soon he shifts, and I feel him wake up. I lift my head and we both see the time on the alarm clock by the bed. It's nearly midnight.

He runs one hand gently down my arm and I shiver happily.

"You're beautiful," he whispers.

"You're not so bad yourself," I say back.

"I can't believe that really just happened," he says. "Was it your—I mean, have you . . . ?"

"My first time," I say.

"Mine too," he says. I wonder if I should be more suspicious and accusatory about the fact that he brought protection, but he claimed he always carried it, and I was so happy to see it that I didn't actually care whether it was a sign of sinister planning or innocent foresight.

There's a pause. I trail a finger along his collarbone. "You know what I'm thinking?" I ask.

"Again?" he says. "Now?"

"You're a terrible psychic," I say, laughing. "I was going to say that I'm really, really hungry."

"Oh, yeah," he says, pretending to sound macho. "Me too. That's what I was going to say. What did you think I meant?"

"Should we go looking for food?" I ask.

"Or," he suggests, pulling me closer, "have them bring it to us."

"Best plan ever," I say, leaning over him to grab the room service menu from the bedside table.

Sofia doesn't call again until midafternoon the next day, Saturday, which leaves us a lot of time for sleeping, ordering room service, watching goofy TV, and certain other things.

Finally my phone rings, and I shoot a guilty look at the crumpled heap of clothes where I left my dress. I wonder if there's a way to get it cleaned before Sofia's wedding, or if I'll have to be a bridesmaid in jeans this time.

"Hey, Sofia," I say brightly into the phone. "The anticipation is killing us over here."

"We're not eloping," she says.

I look over at Leo, who raises his eyebrows inquisitively, and I shake my head. "Oh," I say, trying to sound noncommittal. "How come?"

"Because we're only twenty years old," Sofia says. "We've decided maybe this was a bit sudden. I'll go visit him at Christmas and we'll see how we feel about the future then."

"Oh," I say again, and she starts laughing.

"It's okay, Jack," she says. "If even I have come to that conclusion, I'm guessing you might have had the same thought."

"I told you—I support you no matter what," I say.

"Well, thank you," she says. "I'm sorry this trip was such a waste of time for you."

I look at Leo again. "It wasn't so bad," I say, smiling.

"Would you be ready to fly home tonight?" she asks. "There's an overnight flight we can switch to that'll be cheaper."

"Oh . . . sure," I say, hoping she can't hear my disappointment. Being with Leo on our own in a hotel room in Vegas is one thing. Once we're home again . . . I don't know what might happen.

"Okay," she says. "Meet you in the lobby at seven."

I flip the phone shut. "The wedding's off."

"That's good, right?" Leo says.

"I think so," I say. "She sounded happy about it. We have four hours, and then we're leaving."

"Four hours?" he says, and I don't miss the disappointment in his voice, too. "Then . . . we'd

268

better make the most of it." He takes my hand and pulls me, laughing, onto the bed.

Everything seems to be going well—Sofia and Ben are still acting cute and happy with each other, instead of mad, like I thought they'd be, and we make it to the airport in plenty of time for the overnight flight. Leo and I play Uno on the plane until I fall asleep on his shoulder. It isn't until we get to the airport at home and have to say good-bye that things start going wrong again.

While Sofia and Ben wait by the baggage claim, I walk Leo over to the elevator to the parking lot. He stops, takes my hand, and says teasingly, "So does this mean I can be your date to Paris's wedding next weekend?"

"Yeah, right!" I joke back. "Maybe if we're hoping for a natural disaster."

There's an awkward silence, and when I look up, he has a hurt expression on his face.

"Leo," I say, "I thought you understood. Why would you want to ruin everything now? I mean, Vegas is one thing, but . . ."

"Then what was all that?" he asks, dropping my hand and stepping back. "Didn't it mean anything to you?"

"Of course it did," I say, although my brain is screaming, *Act casual! Don't let him know how much you care! You'll just get hurt if you do!* "But now we're going back to the real world." *Where things can go really wrong. Especially with one more, completely insane wedding to go.*

"Jack," he says, and for the first time I hear anger in his voice. "I'm crazy about you, and you know it. I don't care if you think it's stupid—I believe in love at first sight, and I believe you and I would be great together. Or at least, I did . . . but you clearly don't feel the same way, or, you'd be like me—you wouldn't let anything come between us."

"But—"

"I've been patient," he says. "This whole summer. Haven't I? I did what you wanted—I followed your rules. I was going to do that in Vegas, too. I didn't want to push you; I thought I could wait forever for you. But *you* kissed *me*,

Jack. You—I just—I don't understand you."

"Leo," I start to say, but I don't know what I'm going to say next, and he doesn't give me the chance.

"Please . . . don't," he says, turns, and walks away.

I feel like my heart has just been kicked out of my chest. Our banter has always been fun and flirty, never serious. To see him like this is a shock. It makes me realize that this isn't just a game to him, either.

I didn't think it was possible to feel worse than I did after David broke up with me, but this is infinitely worse. This is exactly the kind of pain I wanted to avoid—the pain I knew would be inevitable if I gave in and let myself feel this strongly for Leo.

But all this time, I've been worrying so much about getting hurt . . . it never occurred to me that I could hurt him, too.

We can actually hear the shouting from the street as Ben pulls up in front of the house to drop us off.

"Um," Sofia says, "this might not be the best time for you to come in, Ben."

"Thank you for sparing me," he says, kissing her lightly. "Call me later?"

"You bet," she says. Now why couldn't my good-bye with Leo be more like that? I mean, I'm not the one who called off a wedding this weekend . . . you'd think Sofia and Ben would be the ones fighting. Sigh.

Sofia and I give each other nervous looks as Ben pulls away.

"I have to admit, Sofia," I say, "I'm kind of glad we're not about to go in there and tell them you're suddenly married."

"That might have been awkward, huh?" she agrees with a laugh.

"NOBODY IN THIS FAMILY CARES ABOUT ME!" we hear Paris bellow, and there is an almighty crash. "NOBODY SUPPORTS ME, NOBODY CARES WHAT I WANT, AND NOBODY UNDERSTANDS WHAT I'M GOING THROUGH!"

Dad shouts something in return, but we

can't make out the words, because he doesn't have quite the volume of dear Paris. Sofia takes my hand, and with a deep breath, we climb the steps and walk through the front door.

Paris is up on the balcony that overlooks our front hall, flinging things over the edge. I notice there are overalls and leotards scattered about, in addition to sunflower flip-flops and sunflower hair clips and a box that was probably the crash we just heard.

"YOU!" she shouts in a melodramatic voice, spotting us. Her bright yellow hair is sticking out wildly in all directions. "I can't believe you did this to me! And I was going to give you TRIV-ETS!"

I glance at Sofia to see if this mysterious statement means anything to her, but she looks as puzzled as I do. Dad pokes his head over the stair rail and sees us.

"Would you tell Paris that she's being irrational?" he says. "It is entirely unnecessary for each of her guests to have an individual miniature homemade chocolate soufflé."

"But it would be ADORABLE!" Paris yells. "WHY DON'T YOU WANT MY WEDDING TO BE *ADORABLE*?"

Dad sighs heavily and rubs his forehead. "I'm glad you girls are home. You talk to Paris. I'll be in my office. For the next five years."

He vanishes down the hall and Paris glowers at us from the balcony above. I think we're quite lucky she's already thrown the box over, or it might have been aimed at our heads right about now.

"You are *out*," Paris declares. "You *abandoned* me in my hour of need. And so you can say good-bye to your cute outfits"—she points dramatically at the overalls—"to the adorable hairdos . . . and to the one-of-a-kind Paris original trivets I was going to give you as your bridesmaid presents! Well, not anymore! You're going to have to wear your own stupid clothes to my wedding! Because now I know who my only real sister is, and it certainly isn't either of you!"

She flounces dramatically down the hall upstairs and we hear the door to her room slam.

"I wonder what that means," Sofia says, poking the overalls with one toe. "You think Alex or Sydney made a comeback this weekend?"

"If it means they end up in the overalls instead of me, I'm going to be just heartbroken," I say.

Sofia crouches beside the box and peeks inside. "Oooh," she says. "Wait'll you see this." She pulls out a twisted, copper-colored metal thing that looks a bit like a squashed bird's nest.

"Oh no—a one-of-a-kind Paris original trivet!" I say, pressing one hand to my heart. "I'm truly crushed."

Sofia grins. "Okay, now we're just being mean. We should probably go apologize to her."

I look regretfully at the sunflower flip-flops. "Are you sure we can't apologize *after* the wedding?"

"Don't bother," Mom says, bustling in from the kitchen with flour in her hair and all over her hands. "We don't have time for you to apologize or for you to be bridesmaids, anyway. Sofia, I need you to run out and buy me twenty

Mason jars, as cheap as you can find them. Paris wants wildflowers with the sunflowers for her centerpieces. And Jack, you're in the kitchen with me—we're making two hundred large sunflower cookies, which will be just as cute as miniature chocolate soufflés!" Mom shouts this last part at the upstairs, so I get the impression it's not really intended for me.

"BUT I WANT SOUFFLÉS!" Paris screams from inside her room. "WHY DOESN'T ANYONE EVER DO WHAT *I* WANT?"

Mom rolls her eyes, seizes my wrist, and drags me into the kitchen, which is a sea of pans and baking sheets and mixing bowls. She shoves a recipe book at me and commands: "Read."

The rest of the day is a blur. We didn't sleep very much on the plane, and to be honest I didn't sleep much the night before either, so I follow Mom's instructions in a sort of daze—measuring, mixing, rolling, and pressing sunflower-shaped cookie cutters into the dough. While half my brain is doing that, the other half is thinking about Leo. This would be much more fun with him here. This whole summer—all the wedding craziness—has been bearable only because of him.

Have I ruined everything?

Is there any way to get him back?

Once the dough is stashed away in the refrigerator and Mom finally releases me, I stagger back to my room and collapse on the bed without unpacking or changing. Instead I pull out my cell phone and dial Leo's number. It goes straight to voice mail, and I realize I have no idea what to say, so I hang up, feeling like a coward.

"Maybe I should just elope!" Paris hollers out in the hallway. "That would teach you all a lesson!"

Chapter Seventeen

The week flies by, and there's no sign of Leo. Carolina stops by often, but always without him, and I'm too chicken to ask where he is, in case he told her about the whole situation. We're so busy, I can almost keep my mind off him sometimes. Paris claims to be so furious at us that there's no chance she'll let us back into the wedding party, but, mysteriously, we're still working as hard as we would if we were bridesmaids. Paris behaves as if we are doing penance for our sins and should be grateful she's letting us be involved at all.

"Remember," Sofia whispers to me, "in a week she'll be married, which means she'll be gone for a month on her honeymoon, and then she's moving to New York with Jiro. Just hang on until then."

Monday's project is the wedding program, which of course turns out to be much more complicated than necessary. Paris wants it printed on bright yellow paper, folded in half with a dark green ribbon tied around the fold. She also wants a photo of her and Jiro on the front cover, but since there isn't a good photo of them together, he has to take the train out from New York first thing so that Sofia can follow them around the yard with the digital camera until Paris is finally satisfied, at which point he is stuffed right back on the train and sent home again.

Then she has a long debate with herself (and, unfortunately, us) over whether to cut scalloped edges on all the programs. She also insists on mentioning somewhere in it that she did all the catering and the flower arrangements for the wedding—this despite the fact that I don't actually see her set foot in the kitchen most of the week. I gather she thinks that *demanding* a particular menu is the same as "catering" it.

And she also has to call Jiro several times to get the correct spellings of his various relatives' names, which takes a million years because each time the two of them talk there is much more in the way of smooching noises than actual information-exchanging.

"My, my," Paris says pointedly, clicking around with the mouse as she designs the program—on my computer, I might add. "Look at all this extra *space* I have. It's funny how much you can fit in when you don't have to list a whole bunch of ungrateful *bridesmaids*."

It takes us half the day to get them printed and the other half to fold them all and tie the ribbons, especially since Paris keeps insisting we're doing it wrong and making us retie the bows. That night I try Leo's phone again, and once again he doesn't answer.

Tuesday we work on place cards—writing them out by hand in dark green marker, rewriting them when Paris changes the seating arrangements for the hundredth time, and clipping them into the sunflower card stands she bought online somewhere.

Tuesday afternoon, just as we're finishing those up, Paris suddenly remembers that she doesn't have a guestbook, which sends her into a panicking meltdown.

"I HAVE TO HAVE A GUESTBOOK!" she hollers, running up to her room to get her shoes. "It won't be a real wedding without a guestbook! I have to be able to remember it forever and always!"

"If she drinks as much as she did at Sydney's wedding," Sofia murmurs to me, "she'll need lots of help to remember it all."

Paris comes slamming down the stairs again and grabs my wrist. "Come on, Jack. If we can't find the perfect one, we'll just have to make one ourselves."

The prospect of spending a whole afternoon doing that gets me moving pretty quickly. Paris insists on going to pretty much every stationery store within a seventy-mile radius, and of course, in the end we go back to the very first one, which has a plain white book that Paris decides she can gussy up with sunflower decals to make it more "thematic." She actually buys three, just in case she messes up the decorations on the first one, and we spend the rest of the night "helping" her decide which one to use.

Leo doesn't answer his phone Tuesday night either. This time I muster up my courage and leave a message: "Hey, Leo. It's, um, it's Jack. I'm sorry—I don't know what to say. But I am sorry. Can we maybe talk about it sometime?" Yeah, it's not exactly inspired. I'm not surprised when he doesn't call me back.

On Wednesday Mom has us make the food that'll keep in the fridge until Saturday, namely, buckets of potato salad, the rest of the sunflower cookies, truckloads of fruit salad, and a baked ziti dish that Mom plans to reheat the morning of the wedding.

While we chop potatoes and slice strawberries, Paris perches on the counter beside us and works on her wedding vows, which apparently involves a lot of sighing, wistful gazing into the air, and stealing of sliced strawberries.

Alex stops by to help us in the kitchen, but Paris is as chilly as she has been since they fought at Vicky's bridal shower, and Alex doesn't stay long. I guess that means it's Sydney who was upgraded to "good sister" in our absence, although she certainly doesn't show it by turning up to do wedding things at any point.

"I don't *knoooooooow*," Paris moans, banging her head (not hard enough, if you ask me) on the overhead cabinets. "I mean, 'in sickness and in health' just sounds so *gross*, you know? It makes me think of *boils* and *vomit*."

"Paris, please," Mom says, eyeing the giant bowl of potatoes and mayonnaise. "Not in the kitchen."

"Is Jiro writing his own vows, too?" Sofia asks.

"Of course!" Paris flicks her forelock of hair back with a smug look. "I mean, I want to know what he thinks of me, after all."

"Well, this seems like a good time to find out," I say, and give Paris an innocent look when she glances at me suspiciously.

The phone rings, and I nearly impale myself on the strawberry-slicing knife as I leap for it, but Paris gets there first.

"Hi, Carolina!" she trills. "No, we're not busy." Sofia rolls her eyes at me. "Sure, I'll be there soon." She hangs up and pops off the counter. "I wonder what happened to her cute assistant," Paris muses as she gathers her purse off the counter. "It's like he just vanished."

Sofia gives me a hard look as Paris sails out of the kitchen, but I don't meet her eyes. As soon as I can slip away, I try calling Leo again.

"I wish you would answer," I say to his voice mail. "I miss you, Leo. Please . . . please talk to me."

But my phone is silent for the rest of the day.

On Thursday, Paris completely loses her mind. She bursts into my room at six o'clock in the morning. SIX O'CLOCK IN THE MORNING.

"It's the end of the world!" she wails. "We're

doomed! Everything is ruined! RUINED!"

"Oh, that's terrible," I mumble, burrowing farther under the sheets.

"SOFIA!" Paris screams, flinging herself down on the floor in a dramatic heap. After a moment, I hear my other sister's door open, and she stumbles blearily into my room.

"What's the emergency?" she says with a yawn.

"Just the end of the *world*, that's all," Paris declares hysterically. "My wedding is going to be totally *destroyed*."

Sofia climbs into bed beside me and steals one of my pillows. Her feet aren't too cold yet, since she just jumped out of her own bed, so I allow this. "Tell us what's going on, Paris," she suggests, lying down.

"Only a HURRICANE, that's what," Paris announces. "A freaking HURRICANE heading RIGHT FOR MY WEDDING, that's what!"

Well, that wakes me up a little. "Seriously?"

"That's what the Weather Channel says!" Paris sits up, her eyes wild. "I might as well just cancel my wedding right now!"

"Sweetheart, if we lived our lives according to the Weather Channel, we'd probably never leave the house," Sofia points out sensibly.

"But if there's a hurricane in the middle of my wedding, it'll be the worst thing that's ever happened to anyone EVER!"

"Maybe we should just keep an eye on it and see what happens," Sofia suggests. "And come up with an alternative in case it does rain." This, by the way, is something Mom and Carolina have both been suggesting since day one, to no avail.

"No!" Paris shrieks. "I'm getting married on that beach or NOT AT ALL!" She springs to her feet and storms out of the room, which would probably be more dramatic if she didn't have to navigate around my piles of clothes and trip on a stack of books on the way out.

"Did you hear that?" Sofia says to me. "A natural disaster is heading our way. And, oh, wait . . . are you dating anyone right now? Or is this happening completely independent of you?"

"Shut up," I say, shoving her out of bed.

"Just think about that," she says, and wanders back to her own room.

I wrestle with my conscience for a while, and then decide that maybe if he's fast asleep, Leo will answer the phone without realizing who's calling. But of course, it goes straight to voice mail again.

"Did you hear about the hurricane?" I ask. "It's like the universe thinks we're together anyway. So . . . maybe we should be. Please? Leo? Can't we at least talk?"

With a sigh, I hang up and try to go back to sleep. But all I can think about is Leo's face as he walked away at the airport, so eventually I get up and go help Mom make guest folders for all the hotel rooms with directions to the wedding site.

Friday is the craziest day of all. By now, I miss Leo so much it's like every cell in my body is urging me to run off and go find him, and I probably would if Mom and Paris didn't have an iron grip on me the whole day. We (meaning me and Sofia) have to pick half of the wildflowers (the rest can't be picked until tomorrow morning) and start arranging the centerpieces, which creates an almighty leafy mess all over the deck, and we have to go out to the park and meet with the rental people who are setting up the tent so we (meaning Paris) can be sure that it's situated exactly right for a perfect view of the ocean with tables exactly arranged around the dance floor they lay down for her.

We also have to listen to every single song on Paris's iPod so she can decide what order she's going to play them in, and we have to test out the speakers she's rented to plug her iPod into, and then we have to listen to the whole wedding playlist over and over again for the rest of the day, which at least features less annoying music than Vicky's, but also has an odd overabundance of Ludacris that I'm sure my parents' elderly friends are going to be thrilled about.

And of course, Friday night is the rehearsal dinner, where we finally get to meet Jiro's parents for the first time. They also seem like sweet, quiet people, as baffled by Paris and the whole wedding thing as the rest of us are. Jiro's mom speaks a little English, enough to make reservations for just the family at the nicest Chinese restaurant in town.

Much to my surprise, Victoria and Kevin join us, and Paris doesn't drive them away. Alex and Harvey, Sydney and Marco, Sofia and Ben—everyone has someone but me. I thought that was how I wanted it, but I really miss having someone I can whisper snarky comments to and whose hand I can hold under the table.

I kind of wish Paris had set me up like Victoria did, but Paris cares much less about symmetry than Victoria does. As long as all the attention is on her, Paris doesn't really worry about what everyone else is doing.

Mom and Dad give a pretty restrained toast—holding back, I'm sure, for the sake of Jiro and his parents. Jiro's mom also gives a short "best of luck" kind of toast. Outside, the wind is picking up, but it hasn't started raining yet. Paris steals Alex's BlackBerry several times to check for weather updates, her face getting paler and paler each time.

I sneak off during dessert to call Leo one more time, again with no success.

And then, finally, the longest week of my life is over, and it's Saturday morning.

The day of Paris's wedding has arrived at last.

Chapter Eighteen

I open my eyes slowly. Sunshine is pouring in my window and spilling across my sheets.

The house is suspiciously quiet.

I rub my eyes, and then my ears, wondering if I've gone deaf. There's no screaming; no sounds of Paris freaking out or something going horribly wrong. I squint at the alarm clock by my bed.

It's ten o'clock. Wow. I've actually slept for a decent eleven hours, probably for the first time all summer.

Where is everyone? Why isn't the house full of chaos and panic?

I slip on a pair of socks and pad to my bedroom

door, poking my nose into the hall. It's quiet; all the doors are still shut. But I can smell coffee brewing in the kitchen, so I head down there to see who's up.

Mom and Carolina are sitting at the breakfast table, working on a crossword puzzle. They each have a cup of coffee and an English muffin with jam. It's such a peaceful, ordinary scene that I wonder if I slept through the whole wedding and now it's Sunday.

"Good morning, Jack," Carolina says softly, spotting me. Mom looks up and smiles, putting one finger to her lips to signal me to keep quiet.

"There's coffee over there," she whispers, pointing.

"Why are we whispering?" I whisper back, getting out a mug and pouring sugar into it. I like my coffee to be two-thirds milk and one-third sugar, with a little coffee added for flavoring.

"Paris is still asleep," Mom says with a gleeful expression.

"Isn't it lovely?" Carolina says. "I often find

that the most anxious brides work themselves into such a state that they crash the night before the wedding, sleep beautifully, and wake up completely refreshed and ready for anything."

"Really?" I say, sitting down beside them. This certainly didn't happen with any of my other sisters. It hardly seems fair for it to happen to Paris, although I suppose it's easier on us this way. "What about the hurricane?" I ask.

"Supposedly it's still coming," Mom says, "but right now it's lovely outside." She nods at the sunlight cascading through the patio doors.

A rustle in the doorway makes us all jump nervously, but it's only Sofia, who gets herself a banana and comes to sit with us. "This is so exciting," she whispers. "I wonder when she'll wake up."

"Well, she's doing her own hair and make-up," Carolina says. "And she knows what she's wearing, so she only really needs an hour to get ready. Everything else we have to do will probably go smoother if she sleeps through it." She winks at us.

293

"What would you girls like to do first?" Mom asks me and Sofia. "Food or centerpieces? Someone should go pick the rest of the wild-flowers."

"And you should do it before showering," Carolina says, wagging her head. "You don't want the pollen all over you."

"We can do that, right, Sofia?" I say.

"Sure!" She jumps up, and Carolina points us to two large baskets sitting by the back door.

"These are the flowers we're looking for," she says, giving us a list with photos of each flower beside it. It includes black-eyed Susans, Queen Anne's lace, daisies, and buttercups, along with different kinds of acceptable leaves and ferns. "Be back in an hour, if you can."

It's a strange feeling to be out in the woods behind our house on the morning of one of my sister's weddings, picking flowers like we're in one of those old English storybooks about fami-lies and picnics and May Day and the seashore. Sofia and I look for the brightest colors and the biggest blooms, filling our baskets with bursts of yellow and white.

"What a pretty day," Sofia says. "It's hard to believe there's a hurricane only a few hours away."

"With this family's luck, it'll hit right as Paris walks down the aisle," I say.

"Even if you're still single at that point?" Sofia says pointedly.

I sigh. "Well, it doesn't seem like I'll have much choice about that anyway."

"So what happened with Leo?" she asks. "You guys seemed so happy on the plane, and then suddenly . . . poof, he's gone. He didn't dump you like David did, did he? Because there has been surprisingly little crying and moping and lying around in the dark listening to Sarah McLachlan if he did."

"Hey!" I protest. "I was fifteen! I think my moping has evolved a little since then."

"So you *are* moping?"

"But he didn't do anything," I say. "It was me. I told him we couldn't be together." I tell her the whole story of Las Vegas and our fight at

the airport. At the end she stares at me disbe-
lievingly.

"And you just let him go?" she says. "Just like that?"

"No!" I say. "I've tried calling him every day this week. I've left messages . . ."

"Jack," Sofia says firmly, "do you love this guy or not?"

My mind flashes to Leo bringing me wedding cake samples . . . finding silk flowers to put in the bouquet . . . dancing with me . . . waiting in the car with me outside Yolanda's apartment . . . calling me observant, and beautiful, and all the other wonderful things he's said to me this summer, and how he's always been there for me and tried to take care of me, no matter how ridiculous I was.

"I do love him," I admit, my voice cracking. "He's the greatest guy in the world."

Sofia grabs the basket out of my arms. "So get over there right now and tell him that."

"What?" I take the handle and try to tug it back. "No, I can't! We have a wedding today! I have bridesmaid duties!"

"No, you don't," Sofia says, yanking the basket out of my reach. "You're not a bridesmaid anymore, remember? And I think you've done quite enough for this wedding. You go tell Leo right now that you want him to be your date to Paris's wedding." I open my mouth to speak, and she yells, "Hurricane or no hurricane! Go!"

Well, how can I argue with that? I turn and begin running through the trees. As I get closer to our house, I see Mom and Carolina through the patio doors, puttering around the kitchen. If I go in there, I'll definitely get snared into another task. There's no way to sneak past them and shower or change. I'll have to go to Leo's as I am, in tattered jeans, a black tank top, and the old plaid shirt my Dad wore while he painted the attic. But this is not the time for vanity! This is the time for action!

Luckily my bike is leaning against the side of the garage, where I left it a couple of days ago. I swing onto it and sail out of the driveway without anyone noticing me. It takes me about fifteen minutes to bike to Leo's house, and as I drop my bike on the grass out front, I hope my face isn't too red and my hair isn't too ridiculous.

I ring the doorbell and wait, rolling up the sleeves of the shirt and feeling my heart pound. Is he here? Will he answer the door? Will he see it's me and pretend not to be home?

After a long, long time, I hear the locks being turned, and the door slowly swings open. My heart leaps in my chest when I see Leo standing there, and I realize how painfully much I want to throw myself into his arms.

He's wearing a T-shirt and shorts, and his hair is still tousled with sleep. He tilts his head and squints at me.

"Is it a wedding emergency?" he asks. "Did my mom send you?"

"No," I say. "I—"

"Wait, let me guess—Paris has decided she wants a horse and carriage to take her away after the wedding, and we absolutely must find one in the next three hours. Am I right?" He actually smiles a little, and I smile back.

"Nope. Nobody knows I'm here. Well, except

Sofia. I'm a runaway bridesmaid. Or, you know, ex-bridesmaid." I get the impression I'm babbling.

"Ah," he says, leaning against the doorframe.

"It's not about the wedding," I say. "Except—" I take a deep breath. "I was wondering if you wanted to be my date. To Paris's wedding. This afternoon."

His eyebrows arch. "Seriously? What about The Curse?"

"I don't care," I say boldly, looking him straight in the eye. "It doesn't matter what happens. I would rather be set on fire again than lose you."

The corner of his mouth twitches. "Hopefully that won't be necessary."

"So you'll come?" I say. "Please? Will you?"

He looks down at his feet. "I don't know, Jack. Maybe I was wrong about all this."

"No!" I cry, seizing his hand without thinking about it. "You weren't, really, I swear. I feel the same way you do, I really do. I—" My voice catches in my throat, but I force it through. "I love you, Leo."

He squeezes my hand and meets my eyes again. His are so green, it's like looking into sea glass. "Just . . . let me think about it, okay?" he says. "I need to think."

"Okay," I say as he drops my hand. "If there's anything I can do to convince you . . . you know, there's going to be sunflower cookies. And I'm pretty sure Paris is going to play her entire Pink collection when it comes time for dancing. And hey, if we're lucky, there'll be a hurricane. You don't want to miss that, right?"

He half-laughs. "Okay, I'll let you know."

"All right . . . bye then," I say.

He shuts the door, and I'm left with a peculiar ache in my chest that I can't do anything about. Instead I get back on my bike and ride home, where I find that Paris is *still* sleeping, and Sofia is putting the wildflowers in Mason jars out on the deck. I help her finish that, and we drive them over to the park, where we set out the wildflowers and the sunflowers on the tables (which, to be honest, doesn't leave a lot of room for place settings, but that is what Paris asked for). By the time we get back, it's noon, and time for us to shower and get dressed.

Since we've been spared the overalls, Sofia has offered to lend me one of her sundresses—a cute, knee-length, teal silk dress that actually makes my eyes look a bit more blue than gray. I wear silver butterfly clips to pull my hair back and a silver butterfly necklace.

I'm putting on lip gloss when Sofia comes into my room, wearing a long blue-green dress with hints of gold thread woven into it.

"You look amazing," I say.

"You too," she says with a smile. "You'll knock his socks off."

"If he comes," I say glumly.

"And if he wears socks," she says, pretending to look thoughtful.

"Do you think he will?"

"Wear socks? I would think so."

"No!" I turn around and throw the nearest stuffed animal at her. "Will he come?"

"It doesn't matter," Sofia says, "because you put yourself out there and that's what counts."

"I think it matters a lot," I grumble, turning back to the mirror.

"So . . . do you think someone should wake the bride?" Sofia suggests.

"Um, not It!" I say quickly. "Maybe if I wanted my head bitten off."

Suddenly the doorbell rings, and we both freeze. "I bet that did it," Sofia says. "She'll be tearing out of her room any second now."

"Who do you think it is?" I ask. "Leo? Do you think it's Leo?" I shoot out of my chair and out the door before she can respond, and I get downstairs before Mom has even made it out of the kitchen.

But when I open the front door, it's not Leo at all. It's Victoria. And . . . she's wearing her wedding gown. *What?*

"Um . . . hi, Vicky," I say cautiously. I wonder if it's safe to point out that this isn't actually *her* wedding day, or if she's decided to wreak some terrible revenge on Paris by crashing her wedding as a bride, which . . . seems convoluted, if you ask me.

"Hi, Jack," Victoria says sunnily, swanning

into the front hallway. "Where's Paris?"

"Still asleep," I say, wincing. Victoria's eyes widen.

"My goodness!" she says. "We should do something about that!" And then, as Sofia, Mom, and I watch in astonishment, Vicky sails right up the stairs and down the hall to Paris's room, where she knocks and then barges right in.

"It's time, it's time!" Vicky sings out. "It's your wedding day, time to get up!"

The door closes behind her, and there's silence. We all glance at one another, expecting to hear Paris shouting at any moment—either about Vicky wearing a wedding dress to Paris's wedding, or about the fact that she's slept until two hours before her wedding, or really, about anything at all, because she's Paris, and that's how she normally wakes up.

But the voices from behind Paris's door are low and civilized, and there are no screams of anguish whatsoever.

"We should escape while we can," I say to Sofia.

"Why don't you go over and set up?" Mom says. "There's plenty of stuff you can take with you."

We load Sofia's car with coolers full of ice, soda, beer, and bottles of water, followed by the box of wedding accessories (the guestbook, the place cards, etc.) and a few baskets filled with bags of potato chips and carrot sticks. When we leave the house, about an hour and a half before the wedding is supposed to begin, Paris has still not emerged from her room.

"Maybe she's changed her mind," I say to Sofia as we drive over to the park. "Maybe she's decided not to get married after all."

"Well, she can't blame it on the hurricane," Sofia says. The sky is still clear and blue, with only a brisk wind even hinting at a storm on the horizon. It's enough of a wind to be a pain in my butt, though, since it keeps trying to blow programs into the ocean and napkins off into the trees. As the rental company arrives with Port-a-Potties and chairs for the ceremony, Sofia and I run around and try to pin everything down. I find

the cleanest rock I can to put on top of the programs in the basket. The coolers of drinks get
arranged around the food table, where we stack
the baskets of chips and carrots. We also have dis-
posable cameras to go on each table, and the
place cards need to be arranged around the guestbook on a side table, in such a way that they
don't immediately go spinning off into the sand.

This is a lot harder than you'd think, and
I actually find myself missing Victoria's crazy-
elaborate origami-chopstick-glass-pebbles-vase
ensembles, since at least those couldn't get
blown away by the wind. Just as I finally get A–G
lined up in alphabetical order, a brisk breeze
swoops in and half of them fly away. I'm chasing
after them, barefoot, with my hair flying around
my face, when I hear a laugh behind me.

I turn around and find Leo standing there,
looking like he just stepped out of a movie about
hot young supermodel crime fighters with
hearts of gold.

"Need some help?" he says.

Chapter Nineteen

"Leo!" I cry, throwing my arms around his neck. He hugs me to him, pressing his face into my neck and breathing deeply.

"I hope it's all right that I'm a little early," he says.

"Of course." I step back and smile at him. "Although you do run the risk of being corralled into helping."

"That's what I'm here for," he says with a grin. He bends to pick up a place card and waves it at me. "A classic problem. Not to worry." We gather the rest of the runaways and I put them back in alphabetical order while he brings over two of the wildflower-filled Mason jars, artfully arranging them to block the wind. He also drops a corner flap of the tent to shelter the table a bit more, and of course, this totally works, because he's a miracle worker.

"Thank you," I say, surveying our work. "If it weren't for you, no one would know where to sit."

"And that would be a catastrophe," he says, smoothing my hair.

"Brace yourself for several more," I say as I take the front of his shirt and pull him closer to me. "Because I plan to do *this* no matter what happens." I kiss him on the lips, and he kisses me back. Joy fills me from tip to toe.

Wild honking from the parking lot announces the arrival of Mom, Carolina, Alex, Sydney, and the two servers Carolina insisted on hiring for the day to help with the food, carrying the chocolate fountain that Paris demanded. Leo and I hurry to help set out the dishes, and nobody comments on his presence, although Sofia gives me a grin and a thumbs-up.

Not long after that, Jiro and his family arrive,

and then the guests start appearing one by one. There's no sign of Paris, although Mom assures me that she was putting on her wedding gown when they left the house, so presumably she was still planning on coming at that point. I glance at Jiro, who is fidgeting nervously in the suit that Paris picked out for him. As much as I wouldn't want to be saddled with Paris for a wife, I wouldn't want to be ditched at the altar by her, either. I hope that's not what she's going to do to him.

One of Paris's friends—a tall, reedy, bearded guy who calls himself a poet—got ordained on the Internet, so he's performing the ceremony. He shepherds us all down to the water's edge and has us sit out in the hot sun for about ten minutes while he stands in his white robe in front of us, looking peacefully zoned out.

Then another of Paris's friends—the one who claims to be able to play the harp, so she got drafted into being the ceremony musician—suddenly thrums her strings dramatically, and we all turn around.

Paris is standing at the top of the hill from the parking lot, looking gorgeous in a short white satin dress. She is barefoot and has a miniature sunflower tucked behind one ear, matching the brightly dyed color of her hair and the bouquet of sunflowers in her hands. Her nose ring gleams in the sunlight, and she is smiling wider than I've ever seen her smile before.

She comes slowly through the sand toward us, walking more or less in rhythm with the music from the harp, which actually is harder than it sounds because her friend seems to be playing all the strings at once, with no discernible beat that we can hear.

"Wow, look," Leo whispers to me, pointing out to sea. On the far horizon, there's a dark gray line of clouds. Right now it just looks like a thread, but even as I watch, it gets thicker and longer, coming closer and closer.

"It's the hurricane," I whisper back. He looks at me nervously, and I take his hand. "It's okay. Let it come."

Paris must be able to see it, too, but there

isn't a flicker of worry on her serene, beaming face. She walks slowly up to Jiro and takes his hand. The bearded poet pauses, then launches into his speech.

Unlike my other sisters' ceremonies, this one is mercifully short. I wonder if the officiant can feel the storm creeping up behind him, because he seems to hurry through all the boring bits. It's really very dramatic-looking—where we are sitting, there's bright sunshine and sparkling waves, but off in the distance, the long dark cloud rolls closer and closer.

The funniest part of the ceremony is that Jiro has written his wedding vows in Taiwanese. Paris looks bewildered when he first starts talking, but his voice is so earnest and his eyes are so intent on her that we don't really need to understand the words to guess what he means. So, actually, it's kind of sweet.

Then they are pronounced husband and wife, and we all traipse back up the beach to the tent as the sky gradually turns from bright blue to dark, seething green with gray clouds creeping across it.

"Is it safe?" I ask Dad as we're walking. "I mean, with the hurricane coming?"

"It's not a hurricane anymore," he says. "It got downgraded to a regular storm. So . . . we'll probably get wet, but we should be fine."

"And it's not going to stop us from partying!" Paris cries, overhearing. "Woo! I'm married! WOOO!"

Leo and I hurry under the tent and stand near the dance floor, watching everyone else crowd under as well. Paris has coerced Yolanda into being the DJ, which seems appropriate, since she is the only person I've ever met who can match Paris for volume. Yolanda grabs the mike and booms, "Hey guys, what's happening? We have kind of a cool situation today. I want you to welcome for the first time as a married couple, Paris and Jiro—and for the *second* time, her sister Victoria and her husband, Kevin!"

My jaw drops. So does Sofia's. So does Mom's, and Sydney's, and Alex's. Paris and Jiro sweep onto the floor, hand in hand, and then, as

311

if they just popped out from the trees (which we later find out they basically did), Victoria and Kevin join them, in full wedding regalia, and both couples put their arms around each other and start swaying to Paris's favorite slow song, "Lucky," by Bif Naked.

"I guess that explains why she was wearing her wedding dress this morning," Sofia says to me.

"And who Paris's only 'real sister' is," I joke.

It turns out that while Sofia and I were in Vegas, Paris and Victoria had a reconciliation. Victoria listened to Paris complain about her wayward bridesmaids, and out of gratitude, Paris offered to let Victoria share her wedding reception, since Vicky's was cut short by a certain someone getting set on fire. (And I'm sure Paris said, "That is *so* typical of Jack" as they talked about it, too.)

The next song is the father-daughter dance, a song called "When My Little Girl Is Smiling," by the Drifters, which Dad picked out to surprise Paris with. The lyrics go: "When my little girl is smiling, it's the greatest thrill there can be. She gets her way, it's true—but I know I won't be blue, as long as she just smiles for me." And from the look on Dad's face, I can see it's true. No matter how ridiculous or impulsive or crazy Paris is, she's still his daughter, and he can't stay mad at her when she's this happy.

At last the third song comes on, and Yolanda invites us all onto the dance floor. I grab Leo's hand and pull him forward as "In Your Eyes" starts playing.

"Finally," I say, leaning my head on his shoulder. Outside, thunder rumbles and the heavens open up. Rain pours down from the sky, and Paris's friends run around rolling down the sides of the tent to keep us dry. But the song keeps playing, and I look up at Leo with a smile. Smiling back, he whirls me around, dips me, and then starts to step back.

Suddenly I realize the chocolate fountain is on the table right behind him. If he moves back another step, he'll crash right into it—meaning chocolate all over his suit, all over me, and all over everything except the actual things we

313

were supposed to dip into it.

I lunge forward, grab his lapels, and yank him out of the way just in time. A gust of wind sweeps through, scattering chocolate droplets on the tablecloth below the fountain. But we are chocolate-free, and disaster has been averted.

"You saved me," he says with a grin, touching my face. "Maybe this wedding isn't so cursed after all."

"It's not," I say, standing on tiptoe to kiss him. "It's perfect." He lifts me off my feet and spins me slowly as we kiss, lightning and thunder crashing outside. Bring on the seagulls and the mumps and the chaos. As long as I'm with Leo, I know we can handle anything.

So maybe being a bridesmaid four times (nearly five!) in three years wasn't so bad. If all that insanity hadn't happened, I would never have met Leo. And if anyone can make me reconsider my position on weddings . . . well, ask me again in, like, ten years, and we'll see.

"In Your Eyes" would make a pretty good first dance song, though. . . .

Picture Perfect

BY CATHERINE CLARK

"I can't *wait* to see all the guys."

You might have thought that was me talking, as I headed into the town of Kill Devil Hills, North Carolina, my destination for a two-week summer stay on the Outer Banks.

But no. It was my dad, of all people.

And it's not what you might be thinking *now*, either. He was talking about seeing his best friends from college.

We meet up every few years on a big reunion trip with "the guys," their wives, their kids, and other assorted members of their families—dogs, parents, random cousins, nannies, you name it. I think it's Dad's favorite vacation, because he and his buddies play golf, sit around

1

reminiscing, and stay up late talking every night.

Even though that occasionally gets a little boring, I like going on these trips, because I've gotten to be friends with "the guys'" offspring, who have sprung off like me: Heather Olsen, Adam Thompson, and Spencer Flanagan. I couldn't wait to see all of them. It had been two years since the last vacation reunion for the four of us, which was *almost*, but not quite, long enough to make me forget what an idiot I'd made of myself the last time, when I was fifteen, Spencer was sixteen, and I'd told him that I thought he was really cool and that we really clicked and that I wished we lived closer because then we could . . . well, you get the gist. *Embarrassing*. With a capital *E*. Maybe three of them, in fact. EEEmbarrassing. Like an extra-wide foot that I'd stuck in my mouth.

But enough about me and my slipup. I basically love these trips because we end up in cool locations like this, a place I'd never seen, or even gotten close to seeing, before now.

"This is just *beautiful*," Mom said as we

turned off the main four-lane road, and onto a smaller road with giant three- and four-story beach houses on each side of it. "Isn't it, Emily?"

We were getting close to the house number we were looking for when Mom shrieked, "Look! There's the house!"

My dad slammed on the brakes, which screeched like the sound of a hundred wailing— and possibly ill—seals. Dad has this awful habit of calling Rent-a-Rustbucket in order to save money. Consequently, we end up driving broken-down automobiles whenever we go on vacation.

Dad backed up and turned into a small parking lot behind the tall, skinny house. I immediately recognized all the *L* bumper stickers and Linden College window-clings on the cars in the lot.

"Look!" Mom pointed at a Linden College banner that was hanging off the third-floor balcony, flapping in the breeze. There was a giant green, leafy linden tree on the dark blue banner background, and in the center, a heart-shaped leaf with a giant *L* in the middle.

Sometimes my dad's Linden school pride got a little ridiculous—for instance, he couldn't possibly get dressed in the morning (at least on weekends and vacations) without donning some piece of Linden College apparel, and he owns about fourteen different ball caps, some faded and tattered and some brand-new—but since I'd actually be going off to school there in the fall, it was kind of a nice feeling to see the banner.

Dad parked the car with a screech of the brakes and we started to climb out. I closed the door and I swear, a piece of the car fell off onto the pavement.

There was a second or two where I was dreading the inevitable hugging and screaming that went along with greeting everyone.

Ten minutes later, after dumping my suitcase in my room, I stood on the giant back deck, overlooking the ocean. There were houses up and down the beach, all looking pretty similar. On one side of us there seemed to be a large, extended family, complete with lots of young kids, grandparents, and about a dozen beach

4

balls and other water toys floating in their pool.

The house on the other side of us had beach towels lined up on the deck railing, flapping in the warm breeze, a couple of lacrosse sticks, a random collection of Frisbees and badminton racquets strewn on the deck, along with a cooler and some empty cans of Red Bull and bottles of sports drink. Something about it screamed "young guys" to me, which seemed promising, but maybe I was just being overly hopeful—or naive. Maybe it was actually screaming "old guys who don't recycle."

Down by the ocean, some kids were playing in the sand, building sand castles and moats, while others swam and tried to ride waves on boogie boards.

"I've made a list of top ten Outer Banks destinations. I read eight different guidebooks and compiled my own list," my mom was explaining to Mrs. Thompson when I walked over to them. "We'll need to go food shopping tonight, of course, and make a schedule for who cooks which night."

"Oh, relax, you can do the shopping tomorrow. Things are very casual around here," Mrs. Thompson said to her. "Dinner's already on the grill, put your feet up." She turned to me. "You should go say hi to Adam. He's down there, in the water."

"He is?"

She gestured for me to join her at the edge of the deck. "He's right there. Don't you see him?"

All I could see except for young kids was a man with large shoulders doing the crawl, his arms powerfully slicing through the water. "That?" I coughed. "That person is Adam?"

His stepmom nodded. "Of course."

Wow. Really? I wanted to say. When I focused on him again, as he strode out of the surf, I nearly dropped my camera over the railing and into the sand. "You know what? I think I *will* go say hi." *Hi, and who are you, and what have you done with my formerly semi-wimpy friend?*

I walked down the steps to the beach in disbelief. Last time I'd seen Adam, his voice was squeaking, and he was on the scrawny side—a wrestler at one of the lower weights, like 145. Not anymore. He had muscular arms and shoulders, and he looked about a foot taller than he had two years ago. His curly brown hair was cut short.

You look different, I wanted to say, but that would be dumb. *You look different and I sound like an idiot, so really, nothing's changed.*

Why was it that whenever I tried to talk to a guy, I started speaking a completely different language? Stupidese?

"Emily?" he asked.

I nodded, noticing that his voice was slightly deeper than I remembered it. It was sort of like he'd gone into a time machine and come out in the future, whereas I felt exactly the same. "Hi."

He leaned back into the surf to wet his hair. "You look different," he said when he stood up.

"Oh, yeah? I do?" *Different how?* I wanted to ask, but that was potentially embarrassing. Different in the way he did? Like . . . sexy? I waited for him to elaborate, but he didn't. "Well, uh, you do, too," I said.

7

"Right." He smiled, then picked up his towel and dried his hair. As he had the towel over his head, I took the opportunity to check him out again. Man. What a difference a couple years could make.

Labor of Love

BY RACHEL HAWTHORNE

"*I* see a spectacular sunrise."

An icy shiver skittered up my spine, and the fine hairs on the nape of my neck prickled. I know my reaction seemed a little extreme, but . . .

When Jenna, Amber, and I walked into the psychic's shop, we didn't tell her our names. So Saraphina had no way of knowing my name is Dawn Delaney.

Sunrise . . . dawn? See what I mean? It was just a little too spooky. It didn't help that I thought I saw ghostly apparitions in the smoky spirals coming from the sharply scented incense that was smoldering around us.

Although I certainly didn't mind that the psychic considered me spectacular. If the sunrise she mentioned was really referring to me—and not the sun coming up over the Mississippi River. Her words were vague enough that they could apply to anything or nothing.

I'd never had a psychic reading before, so I wasn't quite sure how it all worked. I was excited about discovering what was going to happen, but also a little nervous. Did I really want to know what was in my future?

My hands rested on top of hers, our palms touching. Her eyes were closed. I'd expected a psychic to be hunched over and old—wrinkled, gray, maybe with warts. But Saraphina didn't look much older than we were. Her bright red hair was barely visible at the edges of her green turban. Her colorful bracelets jangled as she took a firmer grip on my hands and squeezed gently.

"I see a very messy place. Broken. Boards and shingles and . . . things hidden," Saraphina said in a soft, dreamy voice that seemed to float around us.

Okay, her words calmed my racing heart a little. We were in New Orleans, after all. I didn't need a psychic to tell me that areas of it were still messy, even a few years after some major hurricanes had left their marks.

"I hear hammering," she continued. "You're trying to rebuild something. But be careful with the tools. You might get distracted and hurt yourself—more than hitting your thumb with a hammer. You could get very badly hurt. And worse, you could hurt others."

Not exactly what I wanted to hear. I wasn't even sure if I truly believed in the ability to see into the future, but I was intrigued by the possibility.

If you knew the future, should you accept it or try to change it?

"Lots of people are around," she said. "It's hot and dirty. There's a guy . . . a red and white

11

baseball cap. The cap has a logo on it. Chiefs. Kansas City Chiefs. I don't get a name, but he has a nice smile."

I released a breath I hadn't realized I was holding.

Then Amber had asked if she'd find love this summer. Since Saraphina's eyes were closed, Amber had winked at Jenna and me, because she has a boyfriend back home. She's been crazy in love with Chad ever since winter break when they first started going out.

Saraphina had said, "Not this summer."

Amber had rolled her eyes and mouthed, "See, I told you. Bullsh—"

"But college . . . one better than you already have," Saraphina finished.

That had been just a little too *woooo-woooo* and had pretty much shut Amber up.

Saraphina released my hands and opened her eyes.

"I see nothing else," she said.

Once we were outside, the heat pressed down on us. Until that moment, I hadn't realized how cold I was. My fingers were like ice. I shivered again and rubbed my hands up and down my bare arms.

"Well, that was certainly . . . interesting," I said.

As we walked along quietly, all of us thinking about the fortune teller's predictions, the aromas of chocolate and warm sugar wafted out of the bakery we were passing.

"Let's stop," Amber said. "Maybe a sugar rush will wipe out the worries about our future."

Once we were seated with our pastries, Jenna leaned forward, her blue eyes twinkling. "I've got a crazy idea. We should go to a voodoo shop and have a hex put on Drew and get a love potion for me."

"No thanks. I'm still freaked out about the psychic reading," Amber said. "I'm not sure if I'm ready for voodoo rituals."

The bakery door opened and three guys wearing sunglasses sauntered in. They looked a little older than us. College guys, probably. It looked like they hadn't shaved in a couple of days. Scruffy—but in a sexy kind of way.

They were wearing cargo shorts, Birkenstocks, and wrinkled T-shirts. They grinned at us as they walked by our table. The one in the middle had a really, really nice smile.

He was also wearing a red cap.

A red cap with a Kansas City Chiefs logo on it.